ose
agic

f... ...was all Cinderella had asked.

As if a spell were unwinding, Mitch kissed her, molding his mouth to hers, seeking entry to deepen the kiss. Like a sorcerer, he made her forget everything but him; like a wizard, he filled her with magic. But Mitch was a man, every hard, burning inch of him pressing against her.

She trembled at the quaking she felt in him. She savored his taste. She felt the thunder of his heart against her own.

Or was it the galloping race of time? For an instant she listened, knowing tonight the only things she and Cinderella had in common were a prince and a fatefully ticking clock....

Dear Reader,

As spring turns to summer, make Silhouette Romance the perfect companion for those lazy days and sultry nights! Fans of our LOVING THE BOSS series won't want to miss *The Marriage Merger* by exciting author Vivian Leiber. A pretend engagement between friends goes awry when their white lies lead to a *real* white wedding!

Take one biological-clock-ticking twin posing as a new mom and one daddy determined to gain custody of his newborn son, and you've got the unsuspecting partners in *The Baby Arrangement,* Moyra Tarling's tender BUNDLES OF JOY title. You've asked for more TWINS ON THE DOORSTEP, Stella Bagwell's charming author-led miniseries, so this month we give you *Millionaire on Her Doorstep,* an emotional story of two wounded souls who find love in the most unexpected way...and in the most unexpected place.

Can a bachelor bent on never marrying and a single mom with a bustling brood of four become a *Fairy-Tale Family?* Find out in Pat Montana's delightful new novel. Next, a handsome doctor's case of mistaken identity leads to *The Triplet's Wedding Wish* in this heartwarming tale by DeAnna Talcott. And a young widow finds the home—and family—she's always wanted when she strikes a deal with a *Nevada Cowboy Dad,* this month's FAMILY MATTERS offering from Dorsey Kelley.

Enjoy this month's fantastic selections, and make sure to return each and every month to Silhouette Romance!

Mary-Theresa Hussey

Mary-Theresa Hussey
Senior Editor, Silhouette Romance

Please address questions and book requests to:
Silhouette Reader Service
U.S.: 3010 Walden Ave., P.O. Box 1325, Buffalo, NY 14269
Canadian: P.O. Box 609, Fort Erie, Ont. L2A 5X3

FAIRY-TALE FAMILY

Pat Montana

Silhouette
ROMANCE™
Published by Silhouette Books
America's Publisher of Contemporary Romance

With love
to Joe and his fast feet,
and to Princess Maggie Rose

 SILHOUETTE BOOKS

ISBN 0-373-19369-6

FAIRY-TALE FAMILY

Copyright © 1999 by Patricia A. McCandless

Look us up on-line at: http://www.romance.net

Printed in U.S.A.

Books by Pat Montana

Silhouette Romance

One Unbelievable Man #993
Babies Inc. #1076
Storybook Cowboy #1111
Storybook Bride #1190
Fairy-Tale Family #1369

PAT MONTANA

grew up in Colorado, but now lives in the Midwest. So far, she's been a wife, mother of four adopted daughters, and a grandmother. She's also been a soda jerk, secretary, teacher, counselor, artist—and an author. She considers life an adventure and plans to live to be at least one hundred because she has so many things to do.

Some of the goals Pat has set for herself include being a volunteer rocker for disadvantaged babies and teaching in the literacy program. She wants to learn to weave and to throw pots on a wheel, not to mention learn French, see a play at the Parthenon in Greece and sing in a quartet. Above all, she wants to write more romances.

A FLAT FIT FOR A FAIRY-TALE FAMILY

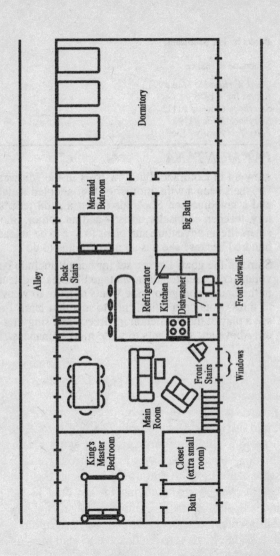

Prologue

Someone was sleeping in her bed. Ellie Sander hugged her daughter closer and backed carefully from the doorway of the moonlit room.

What should she do? Call the police? She'd have to wake Rafe to find the portable phone. Wake all *three* boys and try to herd them quietly downstairs? "Quietly" was not part of her sons' little-kid vocabularies. Stand there and scream bloody murder? That was what she felt like doing.

She was so tired. Two minutes before midnight, and she'd just come upstairs from The Old King Kole Music Shoppe to find her four-year-old daughter sleeping with the dog—*again*. The day's receipts from Kendall Kole's store had refused to add up to the same total twice. She hadn't even *started* studying for her final in her dental hygiene class at the community college. And since Kendall's automobile accident four days ago, she and the kids hadn't made it to the hospital to visit him—not even *once*.

Now some jerk had decided to break into all this mess—and catch a few winks on the job? What were the standards of breaking and entering coming to these days?

Ellie tightened her hold around Seraphina's sleep-heavy little body and rested her cheek against her daughter's head. Maybe, if she waited a second or two, some prince would come to their rescue.

Right. Except that all he would find were country-mouse kids and a frazzled mom fresh out of glass slippers. Hardly the makings of a fairy tale.

She let go a slow, silent sigh. Decision time again. Time to take some action. If she just weren't so tired. Her gaze traveled to a jacket hung on the old desk chair. She squinted to make out the letters stitched across the back. *Winterhaven, Colorado.*

Ellie froze. Omigod.

The man in the bed mumbled through a snore.

She leaned forward to stare at him, careful not to step on the squeaky board just inside the door.

Darn, darn, *darn.* How could she have *forgotten?*

The man lay tangled in her daughter's sheets, one arm flung across his face as if to ward off the moonlight flooding through the flimsy white curtains. But his arm didn't hide his dark, wavy hair, tousled like wind-tossed midnight on Seri's pillow. The same dark hair dusted his arms and the planes of his broad chest and tugged her reluctant gaze down the flat ridges of his stomach...to the folds of the sheet.

Ellie scrunched her eyes shut. Her heart pounded. She'd had no idea Mitchell Kole would look like *this.*

He was big. Bigger than his father. Kendall Kole was attractive for an older man, but his son? Darn, this man was truly handsome. In the moonlight he looked almost…magical.

The Prince! He's come to rescue us! Ellie could imagine her daughter's eager proclamation.

Something inside her stirred, something warm and wanting, feelings all but forgotten. As if, for just a moment, she were a woman again—not just an exhausted mother. Her heart thundered.

Whirling from the doorway, she hurried down the hall, carrying her child away from this new danger. She buried her face in the sweet warmth of her daughter's wispy hair, but the scent only brought back painful memories.

Was it just a year ago she'd hidden her tears in her daughter's hug on the most horrible night of her life? Her husband, her rock 'n' rollin' husband, had rocked off the audition stage at Branson, Missouri, and right on down the highway…along with their ailing van and their pitiful savings. Peter had abandoned them! The realization still stunned her.

If Kendall Kole hadn't offered her this job and a place to stay, she didn't know what would have become of her and her kids.

Tiptoeing into the dormitory, she crept to the twin bed nearest the bathroom and nudged her six-year-old son.

"Rafe, go climb in with Michael," she whispered.

The skinny little guy slid his feet to the floor and tugged down his oversize T-shirt. Clutching a portable phone, he curled into the middle bed next to his eight-year-old brother.

With a heavy heart, Ellie watched the two settle in together. It wasn't the first time they'd had to share a bed. She hoped it would be the last.

In the past twelve years, the only good judgment she'd used had been trusting "King" Kole, she thought rue-

fully. That and the decision to stop crying over Peter—
Peter who had thought playing parent was the same as
doing a musical gig. When he was done playing, he just
packed up and moved on.

Ellie lowered her four-year-old daughter into the still-
warm impression of her son, then turned to pull the sheet
up over the two slender bodies in the middle bed, the
small one light-haired, the other darker, like his father.
Stealing to the far bed, she brushed a kiss on the forehead of her oldest son. A small black terrier grinned up
at her from behind Gabe's legs, tail thumping the blanket
softly.

Ellie raised a silencing finger to the dog. "You are as
bad as a doting grandma," she whispered. She hurried
back to the first bed, slipped out of her long skirt and
oversize sweater and slid in beside her daughter.

A dog for a grandmother and a lonely shopkeeper for
a benefactor and substitute grandfather. Things could be
a lot worse. King had become her friend. She knew her
kids loved him.

But now? With his son here, their futures were in
jeopardy again. Mitchell Kole wouldn't be happy when
he discovered his Humpty Dumpty father had taken in
a woman with so many kids she didn't know what to
do. And a dog who thought she was their nanny.

Ellie curled protectively around Seraphina. Seri might
think Mitchell Kole was a prince, but this was hardly a
fairy tale. Just plain old, nitty-gritty reality—four grubby
kids, one single mom trying to give them some stability
while she learned to clean teeth, and a kindhearted wid-
ower with more broken bones than she'd ever known
existed.

Ellie didn't believe in Tinker Bell. She didn't believe

in magic. And no matter how stirring Mitchell Kole looked in his sleep, she sure didn't believe in Prince Charming.

Not anymore.

Chapter One

"Someone's sleeping in my bed!"

Mitchell Kole squinted one eye open long enough to stop the ridiculous dream, the childlike voice that sounded a lot like Goldilocks accompanied by the distinct scent of peanut butter. He didn't even like peanut butter.

Scrunching his eyes shut, he tugged the sheet up around his ears. Not Goldilocks. Just a very little girl with flyaway brown hair standing by the side of his bed in a pink tutu.

"*What the...?*" In one swift motion, he shoved up to a sitting position.

The child scurried to the foot of the double bed, her tutu bouncing like a tugboat in choppy waters. Leaning forward, she rested her elbows in the folds of the bright comforter, cupped her chin in the heels of her hands and stared back at him. The tutu popped up behind her like a limp peacock's tail.

She couldn't be more than—what? Three...four years

old? What did he know about kids' ages? Her finger-nails, he noticed irrelevantly, glowed a bright green.

What the *hell* was a kid with green fingernails doing in *his* room? What was any kid doing here? He didn't even like kids.

"Hello." She studied him curiously, her big brown eyes framed by dark lashes. "I'm Seraphina. You're sleeping in my bed. I slept with Bubba Sue last night."

"I'm sleeping in *your—?*" Mitch stopped himself midoutburst, suddenly aware that everything around him looked...different. He hadn't bothered to turn on a light last night after coming in so late. Too upset from his visit at the hospital. Incredibly none of the changes in the room had tripped him up in the dark.

"That's my dollhouse."

The kid pointed to a strange accumulation of stacked cardboard boxes filling the space next to the door where his electronic keyboard used to sit. Each box was dec-orated like a tiny room. They were all painted a head-ache-inducing shade of pink. Mitch resisted the urge to shade his eyes.

"Those are my animals."

This time she pointed beneath the window where he'd kept his treasured first ski poles. A faded yellow tiger with one ear missing sat there now next to a teddy bear who looked as if he had the mange. Both of them hun-kered down in a pile of crumpled tissue-paper flowers.

The kid must have decided he didn't need help with the rest of the room, because she watched him silently while he took inventory. His Ski Aspen, Ski Vail posters were missing from the walls, replaced with pictures of figures he vaguely recognized as some of the new Dis-ney characters. And the bed he lay on was afloat in more of the same. He had *never* slept in sheets covered with mermaids!

"*Your* room?" he mumbled, scraping a palm up the bristles on his cheek. Somewhere in the distance, children's shouts overrode the steady chatter of morning TV cartoons. He dragged fingers back through his hair, struggling to get awake, searching to make some kind of sense of all of this...this *mayhem.* Through it all he caught the rich aroma of coffee.

Thank god. Evidence of adult-type beings. What were kids doing in his father's place anyhow? *Living* here, from the looks of this room. What the *devil* was going on?

The little girl straightened. With a gesture that reminded him of a queen, she swept her thin bangs to one side.

"My name means *angel,*" she offered, as if she'd read his mind. "But really I'm a princess." She studied him from the foot of the bed with those grave brown eyes.

She looked more like a waif. She was about as skinny as a puppet, and her mouse brown hair stuck out in feathery wisps from a pink thing on top of her head. On closer inspection, he saw that the netting of her tutu drooped, and the straps across her thin little shoulders had shed most of their shiny stuff.

Mitch eyed her warily. For a princess, this kid's treasures looked mighty tattered. But she didn't seem to know. She acted as self-assured and expectant as any royalty *he'd* ever entertained.

In spite of his growing annoyance, Mitch allowed himself a half smile. Such seriousness in one so little. Seemed to him that a kid her size ought to be giggling about something, not looking as if she carried the weight of a kingdom on her shoulders.

But what did he know about kids? Or care?

Grabbing the edge of the sheet, he held it against his bare middle and slid to the side of the bed. He hadn't come all the way back to Missouri to be stalled by a little squirt's solemn face. He had business to take care of. And a plane to catch back to Colorado this evening.

He'd told Jack he would be back in Winterhaven in two days—Jack Winter who'd taken him in when he'd been an angry, *scared* runaway of almost seventeen. Jack had given him a place to stay, a job. His wife, Josey, had given him the courage to call King and tell him where he'd run. Over the years, Jack had become his mentor—and his friend. Mitch wasn't about to let him down.

So... Still clutching the sheet, Mitch swung his feet to the floor. One thing he'd learned teaching skiing at the Lodge: where there was a princess, there was bound to be a king or a queen. He needed to seek a royal audience pronto. Whoever was living with his father could be the answer to his problem.

"Okay, Princess, I'm...Mr. Kole, and I'd like to get up now so—"

"I know. You're The Prince."

"Seri? Where are you? You'd better not be bothering Mr. Kole."

Hell. Mitch pulled the sheet of redheaded mermaids a little higher around him. If he remembered his fairy tales, princesses weren't supposed to catch The Prince in bed naked.

"Seri, I told you not to—" A woman appeared in the doorway. "Oh..." At the sight of him her eyes widened.

Mitch watched color rosy the woman's cheeks. Things were taking a decided turn for the better.

There could be no mistaking Seraphina's mother. This

woman promised everything the funny little princess would someday become. The kid was skinny, but her mother—now here was pleasure to behold. The kind of woman the word "petite" must have been invented for, with feathery hair the color of light ale brushing her shoulders when she moved.

In spite of her size, she acted about as regal as the kid. Even in that long, shapeless dress, and that brown sweater—which had to be a hand-me-down from her grandfather—she still didn't manage to hide a figure that was...lush. It was the only other word Mitch could think of. Or wanted to.

Until he looked into her eyes. They were blue, the blue of Colorado skies. Of columbine flowers. Of deep, cool mountain lakes.

Or an Alaskan glacier. He tugged the sheets closer.

None of her daughter's studious curiosity there. Instead he found wariness—and other feelings he recognized. Anger. Resentment.

She studied him as if he were some form of outer space alien, a very stupid alien who had witlessly landed in her daughter's bed. A state of affairs she definitely didn't approve.

"Go on now, Seri. To the kitchen." She shooed the girl out the door.

Given the same circumstances in his bedroom at Winterhaven, Mitch would have stretched into a slow, sensuous yawn, given the woman a provocative grin...and stood up. But something about this woman made him hesitate.

Her gaze came to a halt at the fistful of sheet he held against his stomach. Her eyes thawed just a bit. Her honey-colored brows ticked upward.

Fascinated, he watched a corner of her pale pink

mouth curve ever so slightly. To his dismay, he felt himself respond. Clearly this was a woman he couldn't unnerve, not even with the threat of six feet of buck nakedness. The thought pleased him.

"Did not!"

"Did, *too! Mo*-om!" Crash!

A dog barked.

Mitch winced.

The woman didn't even flinch, but her gaze refrosted. "Your father didn't tell you about us, did he?"

Obviously a rhetorical question, because she spun out of the doorway before he could decide between a bitter laugh and a fierce growl. He hadn't come here to get turned on by a little bit of a woman, a woman who was apparently living with his father!

Flinging the sheet aside, he slammed his feet to the floor. Just then the kid popped into the room. Mitch lunged back under the concealing mermaids.

"Seri?" The woman reappeared in the doorway. One glance and she grabbed the kid and ushered her toward the door.

"But, Mommy—"

"Let Mr. Kole get dressed."

They disappeared together, but not before Mitch could check her hand. The woman wasn't wearing a ring. The discovery left him teetering between a definite upswing in mood—and pure raw anger.

"Wait! Miss... Ms...." How was it she already had him analyzed and categorized while he hadn't even known she existed? His frustration level shot skyward. "Hey, lady, who *are* you?" he shouted. He didn't like being out of control. He didn't like being so...perturbed by such a...woman.

She reappeared in the doorway. The kid peeked from behind her legs.

"Sander. Ellie. I'm the one who called about your father's accident."

There was that resentment again. That anger.

"I told him we didn't need to bother you, but he insisted."

Mitch scowled into Ellie Sander's rejecting azure eyes. Damn it, she *did* bother him. She bothered him a lot.

"There's breakfast in the kitchen," she announced flatly, then swung out of the room, her hair fanning her shoulders like a silk skirt.

"Just coffee," he shouted after her. "I don't do breakfast."

Damn! He didn't need to growl just because there were still old issues between him and his father. He especially didn't need to watch her retreat—just because he liked the way she moved. He didn't have time for—

For *any*thing. He'd done his duty; he'd flown to his father's deathbed. But when Ellie Sander had called, she'd failed to give him one minor detail. Old "King" Kole wasn't dying.

Last night at the hospital, Mitch had discovered that King was only temporarily inconvenienced—by a cast on one ankle and another all the way up his other leg. And a headache the size of Mount Rushmore. Which he undoubtedly deserved.

Shoving back the sheet, Mitch tugged into his briefs and stalked down the hall to the bathroom, defying an encounter with more princesses along the way.

He'd go see his father—one more time. He'd make arrangements with the hospital for a visiting nurse. He'd contact a temp agency for someone to help run the store. He'd arrange for whatever his father and this woman needed till King was on his feet again. But Mitch wasn't going to stay.

His father had never been there for him when he was growing up. He hadn't been there for his mother when she'd needed him. King had set the example; for once Mitch figured he'd be justified in following it.

But he would be nice to this Ellie Sander, whoever she was. Why such a pretty, pint-size woman like her would move in with his father—?

"Ouch!" He muffled an oath and gave the bathroom door another, more careful kick. Hell, she was clearly strong-willed enough to live with the old man. Which was good, he lectured himself. Because living with his father was exactly what Mitch wanted her to keep right on doing.

Ellie knew the minute Mitch Kole stepped into the kitchen. Even with her back to the door, she could feel his presence, could smell the faint, outdoor scent that slipped into her awareness right through the aroma of pancakes and coffee.

The same way he'd managed to slip into the apartment last night. Thank goodness she'd been downstairs in the store. For once she was even glad Seri had crawled in with the dog.

If Mitch Kole had arrived after Seri and she had fallen asleep in the double bed—? She hated to imagine. Her screams would have sent him scrambling back to Colorado in his Jockeys—if the man even slept in shorts. From the death grip he'd held on the mermaid sheets, Ellie suspected he did not.

The memory of his discomfort gave her a vengeful

sense of satisfaction. It also made her warm. And disturbed.

But from what she knew of Mitch Kole, she wouldn't need screams to get rid of him.

Refusing to look at him, Ellie moved the portable phone away from Rafe and set plates of bear-faced pancakes in front of him and his sister, both of them seated on stools at the counter.

"Eat up, kids. I have to open the store in fifteen minutes."

"Wonder if I could talk you out of a cup of coffee?"

She forced herself to look up at Mitch then. Right away she knew she'd made her second big mistake of the morning, ranking right up there with walking in on him in bed.

He was dressed now, but what undid her wasn't the way his jeans hugged his ski-tightened thighs nor the way his damp hair curled along the edge of his navy turtleneck. It was his smile. His smile made her feel the same way she had last night when she'd watched him sleep. Warm...and wanting.

Darn! She knew that smile—the carefree grin of a charming, persuasive man. She watched it warm his sapphire eyes and deepen the lines around his broad mouth. His teeth shone startlingly white against his ruddy tan. The effect was breathtaking.

Ellie frowned. She'd given up breathtaking years ago. Along with a lot of other things—like teasing smiles and exciting promises. And when the kids had started coming, she'd given up dreams of a close-knit family...and a home...and security...

But she'd learned—oh yes, she'd learned. And she had no doubts that a charming ski instructor, like a charming musician, was not breathtaking. At least not for long. In the real world, there were no Prince Charmings.

"Sugar? Milk? We only have skim."

"Mommy, The Prince wants bearcakes."

Mitch stepped forward. "Coffee'll do. Don't know if I could handle bearcakes." He smiled down at Seri.

Ellie reached into the glass-doored cupboard for a mug, fighting the melting feeling inside, tightening her defenses.

"Gabe? Michael? Time to eat." *Come on, guys. Please show up—fast.*

Sometimes four kids almost overwhelmed her, but when she gathered them around her and looked into their trusting faces, they always gave her strength. Which was what she needed now. King hadn't told her his son was attractive. He hadn't said Mitch had this…appeal! Intuitively, she knew it put them all in danger.

To her relief, Gabe shuffled in from the living room. When he saw Mitch, he stopped.

She watched the two males size each other up, could almost see the hair rise on Gabe's neck as Mitch smiled at him.

Good. She didn't want her kids snagged by Mitch's charm.

Gabe resumed his trek to the end of the counter, his blue eyes filled with uncertain apology, his golden mop of curls almost level with her head.

"I'm sorry we were arguing, Mom," he mumbled. "Here." He handed her a slightly tattered tissue-paper carnation. Head turned away, he leaned stiffly into her hug.

Pride, and a huge dose of regret, shot through her. In another year she'd be looking up at him.

"Hey!" Michael trotted into the kitchen followed by

the dog. "Hey, hi! You must be King's son. Know what? He told us you were coming. Can I ask you something? Will you teach us how to ski? Wanna see my fast feet?"

"Michael…"

He grinned that two-teeth-missing smile she loved so much and met her at the end of the counter, extending his own offering, half-crushed in his hand. Another paper flower, this one pale green and newly constructed.

"Sorry, Mom. I just wanted to—"

Ellie quieted him with a hug, allowing herself the impulse of wanting to protect him. It gave way quickly to the joy of wrapping her arms around his slender body and breathing in his little boy scent of hard play. Michael was as lean and full of energy as Gabe was solid and steady. She needed what she could draw from them both.

But she also knew when to let go. Before Michael could protest, she pulled away, tickling and poking. "*Ooh,* cooties."

Michael giggled, and Ellie breathed a slow sigh of relief. Her sons had come to apologize. Michael had made a *new* "I love you" flower exactly the way she'd taught all of her children on their fourth birthday. And— blessed relief—for the moment Michael had stopped talking.

"Thank you, boys. I love you, too. Love you all." She smiled at her brood of angels and felt a surge of strength. She would never let anything happen to them again. They had finally found a home and a bit of stability…at least for a while. She wouldn't let Mitch Kole threaten their future.

"Climb up, guys. Time for bearcakes."

She laid the two paper flowers on top of the others in the shallow basket on the counter, cherishing this bouquet of love from her children. Then she lifted more plates from the overhead cupboard and filled them with bear-faced pancakes, adding lots of butter and syrup.

Stalling again.

She had to convince Mitch Kole to go back to Colorado. He'd made it clear that he hadn't wanted to come in the first place, so the task shouldn't be too difficult. Gathering courage, she set the plates in front of her sons.

"Eat up, guys."

"S'pose I could get that cup of coffee now?"

"Coffee—?" Omigod. She'd completely forgotten. Rattled by another of Mitch's breathtaking smiles, she poured the mug too full. Steamy brown liquid sloshed onto the counter.

Mitch lifted the mug, and she swiped away the puddle with a cloth, ignoring the inquiring rise of his dark brows. He was watching her too closely. She recognized that look. Once Peter had watched her like that, when she'd been young and rebellious and smitten with his promises. Before they'd had children.

Peter had made her giddy, the way only an eighteen-year-old could feel. Mitch's regard stirred something else, something that made her nervous and self-conscious and short of breath. Something that made her spill coffee and made her heart race. Whatever it was, she knew she had reason to be alarmed.

King had told her Mitch wasn't a family kind of man. She'd already known that kind of man.

"These are my children, Mr. Kole." She presented them to him with a wave of her hand, her protectors, her talismans against whatever weakness it was in her that Mitch's charm touched. She was well aware that four children under the age of ten would ward off just about any kind of man.

He continued to watch her too closely, with just a shadow of a smile. "Call me Mitch."

Ellie regrouped her defenses. "This is Gabe, my oldest. He's ten. Michael's going on nine. Rafe just turned six...." Pride filled her as each of the boys offered a reluctant hand. "...and you've met Seraphina."

"I'm four years old and two months," Seri piped up, holding up four fingers. "We're The Angels," she added. "Gabriel, Michael, Raphael and—"

"Seri!" Instantly Ellie regretted her sharpness.

"We *used* to be The Angels," Seri said softly. "Before..."

Ellie's throat tightened with contrition. "Sweetheart, I'm sure Mr. Kole isn't interested—"

"Oh, but I am." He eased onto the empty stool beside Seri. *"You'll* call me Mitch, won't you, Princess?"

She nodded eagerly.

"Good. Then tell me, who's Bubba Sue?"

"Don't you *know?* Bubba Sue's King's dog."

"King's dog? Well, I'll be a—" He looked down at the little dog curled up under the stools. "I'm surprised her name's not Queeny."

Seri giggled.

With a sinking heart, Ellie watched her wide-eyed daughter warm to Mitch. In spite of Peter's haphazard fathering, Seri missed her daddy. Ellie didn't want her daughter filling his absence with Mitch's easy appeal. She didn't want her hurt all over again.

Like mother, like daughter—both suckers for those Prince Charming types. Ellie would have to teach Seri better. Right after she convinced Mitch Kole to leave.

"Hey, Mom, it's five past nine."

Gabe's too-grown-up voice interrupted her worries. Almost gratefully, she grabbed at the safety of routine.

"Okay, kids, Saturday morning schedule. Michael, kitchen, Rafe, bathrooms, Seri, beds. Gabe, I need you in the store to move boxes. If anybody needs anything, remember the bell."

She hurried to the stairs leading to the shop below, glancing back for one last check. Burners off, pan in the sink, nothing harmful left untended.

Except Mitch Kole.

"We have things under control here, Mr. Kole. You can go visit your father right away. I'm sure he'll be glad you came. Please tell him we'll be there this evening."

Mitch's watchful gaze sent her backing down the stairs. "I—uh—guess we won't see you again, so I hope you have a very nice life in Colorado." She marched down three more stairs. "Now, if you'll excuse us, we have things to—"

The telephone made her stop. Through the stair railing, she watched Rafe snatch the ringing phone from the counter.

He punched it on. "*Daddy?* Oh." The hope in his dark eyes faded quickly. "Yeah. Yeah. Okay." Dejectedly he punched the Off button.

Ellie's heart ached for her son. She had to make Rafe give up that phone—soon. "Who was it, sweetheart? What did they want? You should have let me talk."

"It's okay, Mom. It was just King. He said…*he'll* bring him home from the hospital." He pointed at Mitch.

Ellie lurched back up the stairs. "*Home?* Did he say when?"

"Um…yeah." Rafe laid the phone back on the counter. "I think he said…tomorrow."

Mitch stood outside the doorway to his father's narrow room staring at the high, four-poster bed his mother had loved, trying to ignore the memories. Now was not the time to brood over the past. He had a problem to solve here.

"I thought you'd be at the hospital by now."

Somehow he managed not to turn, though he couldn't mistake Ellie's voice. Or her challenge. "I didn't expect you back from the store so soon." He sure as hell didn't want to see her again now. Especially not *here*.

"The high school kid who works weekends came in early."

Hell, Ellie practically looked like a high school kid herself. Too young to have *four* kids. Too damned young to be living with— *No.* He shoved down the anger. Her relationship with his father was none of his business.

"I thought I'd check the place out first, get an idea of what King will need."

"That's what I tried to tell you at breakfast." Without looking up at him, she brushed past and into the room. "You can go back to Colorado right away. We'll take care of King."

He should be glad she was avoiding him. But heaven help him, he wanted to look into those blue eyes. "You can't take care of him by yourself."

She still wouldn't look at him. "Yes, I can. The kids and I can take perfectly good care of him."

"There's hardly space in this room for one person to move around. He won't be able to get in and out of that bed."

Ellie pulled herself to her full height and turned to frown at him. "We can help him."

"*We?* Who else are you planning to move in here? Ellie, good intentions aren't enough. You're too small, and your kids are...well, they're just kids." Mitch couldn't decide which was worse, standing here fighting over King's care, or fighting his attraction to the woman who slept with him.

Especially when she was so damned valiant. When her lips looked so full and determined. When the top of her head would barely reach his chin even if she tipped her face up to— Why, a man would almost have to pick her up to...

Ellie stepped back. "Why are you trying to intimidate me, Mr. Kole?"

A damn good question. Except that his anger wasn't intimidation, it was self-defense. Because what he really wanted was to kiss her. A most unwise impulse. But then, when had his impulses ever been wise?

"Look, just call me Mitch, okay?"

He saw her back stiffen, her own defenses go up another notch. His anger just kind of collapsed. "Come on, Ellie, call me Rumpelstiltskin if you want, but give Mr. Kole a rest." To his surprise, her eyes warmed— just a little—as they did when she teased her kids.

"Okay. *Mitch.* So why *don't* you want us to take care of your father?"

"Oh, but I do. I just don't see *how.*"

"Look, I've already figured that out, so you don't need to waste your time."

Not so much a waste of time as a waste of emotion. This place stirred too many memories, but the feelings Ellie stirred were far worse. Especially since he had no intentions of doing anything about them. *Especially* under the circumstances.

"Look, correct me if I'm wrong, but I'd guess my father weighs about a hundred and eighty pounds—dripping wet. *Without* casts. There's no way he can get around in here *with* them."

She fixed him with a firm gaze that clearly said, *Get out of my way,* and marched toward the doorway. "We'll move him into the dormitory."

"The dormitory?" He slouched against the frame, not wanting her to go.

She slowed to a stop. "If you'll move, I'll show you."

Unwillingly he stepped back, bowing slightly.

She moved carefully, turning sideways to keep from brushing against him. She trailed a fragrance that was clean and fresh.

How could he resist? How could he let her go without stealing just one sweet brush of those half-opened lips? The thought of her softness against him sent heat humming through his veins. Raising an arm, he blocked the doorway.

Her blue eyes widened with uncertainty. "Um, the dormitory? I think...when you lived here...you called it—" Her voice caught.

"The Jam Room?" he murmured, leaning toward her.

Almost imperceptibly she turned her face up to him. "Yes. The Jam Room," she whispered. Then she froze.

"No!" She jerked away. "I mean, *yes!* The Jam Room." Before he could stop her, she ducked under his arm and disappeared down the hall.

Damn! What had he been thinking? He needed to get King's arrangements made and get out of here. His pulse still hammering, he followed reluctantly through the small kitchen and down the hall of the second flat.

She hurried across the hardwood floor of the long, rectangular room at the end. Keeping distance between them. A whole lot smarter than he was.

"The boys sleep in here now." Nervously she smoothed the plain, unmatched bedspreads on the three twin beds lined up under the back windows.

He tried to ignore her caring gesture. But her touch was everywhere—in the football and race car posters on the walls, in the plastic basketful of balls and dinosaurs and action figures. In the string of paper flowers hanging above the head of each bed.

The Jam Room—where King Kole and his Merry Men had practiced those rare times when his band hadn't been out on a gig. His father had been gone more than he'd ever been home. Gone when a family really needed him. A lot of things besides this room had changed since then.

"We'll put King in Rafe's bed—the one by the big bathroom. Rafe can sleep with Seri."

"What about *you?*"

She seemed to pull farther away from him, hugging herself until she was almost lost in the bulkiness of her brown sweater. A businesslike frown darkened her eyes.

"You're right. I'll move Seri and Rafe into King's room. I should be near to help Gabe and Michael with him at night. I'll stay where I am."

"Where you *are?*"

"With the mermaids."

For an instant, he thought she was teasing. He watched with growing regret as the possibility faded and understanding crept into her face.

"You thought—?" Her eyes narrowed, chilling again to Arctic frost. "You thought I slept with…and yet you tried to—? I sleep with my daughter, Mr. Kole, *not* with your father."

Her shoes snapped like gunshots on the wooden floor. "Your father offered me a job and a place for my kids when I was pretty desperate." She descended on him from across the room. "I suspect it was because he was lonely. Because he doesn't have *much* family of his own.''

Mitch actually felt himself flinch. What was going on here? His father had always cared more about his music than anything else. More than his family.

Ellie stopped right under his nose and glared up at him. ''When you see King, why don't you tell him what you thought about me. Only a man like you would think such a thing. I'm sure he could use a good laugh.'' She swept by him, disappearing through the door.

A man like him? Mitch knew what he was. Too much like his father for anyone's damn good. But at least he would never lose a wife the way his father had. He would never lose a kid. An unmarried man made no promises to break.

So why did Ellie's words sting?

''You sleep with your *daughter?*'' he mumbled after her, unable to muster a heartfelt shout. Last night, in the dark, he'd climbed into bed with Seri's mermaids—naked. Where had Ellie been then?

Worse, what if she *had* been there?

And *why* was she sharing a bed with a restless little four-year-old instead of with his father?

More to the point, no matter where Ellie slept, why the hell did he care?

Chapter Two

"*What* do you think you're *doing*?"

Ellie gasped at the sound of Mitch's sharp voice. She grabbed the TV tighter, but her startled jerk pulled the big black monster right off the edge of the scarred television stand.

Omigod.

"Hang on, Gabe. Michael, Rafe, come here. *Hurry!*"

The two boys jumped up from the living-room floor, followed by the little black dog. Bubba Sue pranced around wagging her tail.

"Come on, guys, grab hold. *Lift!*"

Darn! She'd hoped to have the TV moved by the time Mitch got back from the hospital. She'd show this...this renegade who'd accused her of...of... And after he'd tried to kiss her!

She *wasn't* a kept woman! She and her kids could take care of King. They didn't need help from Mitchell Kole—or anyone.

But the darned TV weighed more than a carton of bricks!

"*Heave,* guys." She shifted her weight, took a wider step and came down on something that *rooollllled....*

"*Ooohh, nooo... The crayoonnns!*"

"Out of the way, kids. I'll take that."

Mitch descended on them from the landing, just barely capturing the TV as it plummeted toward the floor.

Ellie kept right on plummeting.

"*Unnhhh.*" Whatever she landed on imprinted itself, probably permanently, on her backside.

Seri dashed across the room, with the dog hot on her heels, and threw her arms around Ellie's neck. "Mommy!"

"I'm okay, sweetheart." Ellie nudged the licking dog away and hugged her daughter, all the while avoiding Mitch's glare. Her ego hurt a whole lot more than the bruise that would no doubt tattoo her bottom.

"*Good—!*" two very large, very warm hands lifted her to her feet making her feel like a rag doll with a silly, wobbly heartbeat "—because I'd hate to have to wait till you recover to read you the riot act."

Ellie tried to pull away, but Mitch glowered down at her, holding her tight, making her forget she'd ever wanted to escape. His warmth ribboned through her like some kind of magical potion. She watched his eyes change to a cloudy uncertainty, his gaze slide to her lips. Her knees went weak—the same way they had that morning. What was this man doing to her?

Then he stepped back.

But the distance wasn't enough, not nearly enough to stop what was happening to her. The explosions of light. The wanting. She was overheated and out of control because of his closeness. His touch.

Men like Mitch should *never* happen to her.

"Would you please tell me *what* you were doing?" he demanded. "You could have hurt yourself. Or a kid. You damn near dropped the TV."

Ellie smoothed her sweater over her throbbing bottom and prayed her face wasn't flaming. She tried to ignore her confusion.

"We're moving the TV into the dormitory. I thought since King will be on crutches, I'd bring the land mines out here. Fix a safe place for him in there."

"Land mines?" Mitch scanned the room, clearly uncomfortable.

"Toys." Thank goodness for her children. She waved an arm to introduce him to the hazards of child rearing. And to hide her trembling.

Gabe had flopped back on the threadbare plaid sofa with a book and the dog, though he kept a wary eye on Mitch. More books cluttered the floor and the coffee table where Mitch had rested the TV. Michael crouched in front of his cardboard fortress, talking nonstop to a half-dozen army figures. Rafe stretched on his stomach in front of a coloring book and at least a hundred crayons—along with the portable phone. And Seri fussed with her dollhouse boxes, arranging them like an estate near Michael's fortress.

"All this stuff makes walking…difficult. As I've just so cleverly demonstrated." Ellie managed an embarrassed smile. "I don't want King doing what I just did."

She stood a little taller, the movement reflected in the mirror above the sofa. Mitch's reflection caught her attention, too, and she couldn't stop herself from meeting his gaze. He was watching her again with that same meltdown intensity. For a moment her heartbeat threatened to run away.

"Neither do I," he murmured.

Neither did he what? Darn! Now he had her forgetting what they were talking about. Ellie gave herself a swift mental kick. This was the man who'd assumed she was his father's *mistress,* for heaven's sake. The woman staring back from the mirror hardly qualified for *that* kind of job. Clothes hanging too loose, eyes sporting dark circles—and her children, her wonderful children, added up to *four.*

No man took a mistress with four children—Mitch should know that. Her husband hadn't even wanted a *wife* with four children.

She made a point not to look at Mitch again as she headed toward the door. "Okay, guys, let's bring the rest of your stuff out here."

"Since he thinks we're too weak, why don't you have *him* help?" Gabe's defiant voice rose from behind his book.

"Gabriel Sander, that's no way to—"

"I…uh…have a few things to tell you first."

Mitch's announcement stirred Ellie's concerns. "Is King okay? They're keeping him in the hospital longer, aren't they? I didn't think he should come home after only four days." *Please let that be all Mitch had to tell them.* She didn't know how she would deal with anything more.

"He's doing as well as can be expected—for a man who's used to his freedom." A shade of bitterness darkened Mitch's tone.

How could he talk about his father like that? "For a son who hasn't been around in years, you seem to know an awful lot about your father."

For once, Mitch avoided looking at her. "The doctor

said he can come home tomorrow. But there'll have to be more changes around here.''

"Like what?" she demanded.

"To start with, he'll need a hospital bed, one that raises and lowers. And a mattress that'll hold more than a fifty-pound kid. Also, a trapeze bar." Mitch ticked the items off slowly. He looked downright uncomfortable.

Michael jumped up from the floor. "King's gonna have a trapeze? I want to swing on King's trapeze, can I, Mom? Please, can—"

"I bet King will let you." Mitch ruffled Michael's hair.

Ellie eased her son out of Mitch's reach, squeezing his shoulders possessively before she nudged him back to his toys.

"It's not a circus trapeze, Michael. It's for..."

"Exercise," Mitch offered.

"Right." Ellie braced herself, not trusting where Mitch was headed with this information. "I'm sure we can find something in the store to rig one up." Even if she couldn't imagine a man wearing a cast and exercising on a trapeze. "We can double up the mattresses and put Michael and Rafe in King's room."

"The kids won't have to sleep together." Mitch hesitated. "I rented a bed."

"You rented—?"

"It'll be delivered this afternoon. We just have to make room for it."

A bed. To help her and the kids care for King by themselves. Mitch was arranging things so he could go back to Colorado. Suddenly all the wind went out of her defensiveness.

"A bed. Right. There'll be plenty of room in the dormitory for another bed. We'll get the toys out...and move the TV in. You can do that, Mitch.'' She should be saying thank you instead of sounding like the job foreman. She *wanted* Mitch to go back to Colorado. So why wasn't she feeling grateful?

''I don't think you'll have to isolate King from the toys.''

With each of Mitch's announcements, her uneasiness grew. ''Were you planning to tell us why anytime soon?''

''He won't be on crutches for a while.''

''*Why?*''

Mitch inhaled slowly, as if what he had to say came hard.

''They've got him kind of wired together. His right ankle has a pin, and his left shin... Let's just say he'd never make it through a metal detector. Both legs have to be elevated—for circulation. He can't put weight on either leg.''

''You mean he won't be able to get out of *bed?*''

Mitch winced. Then he nodded.

Ellie's hopes plunged—because she *could* imagine King lying in a bed surrounded with railings, both legs encased in plaster casts suspended from the ceiling by ropes, his body swathed in miles and miles of white bandages. Like an accident victim in a cartoon.

But the cartoons never showed the jillion things about which she didn't have a clue. Like shaving a patient...and getting him dressed. And undressed? Like bedsores...and bed*pans?* And baths? How did a person care for a very large, very active, very bedridden...male?

How could *she* and four little kids possibly do it?

Mitch watched worry spread across Ellie's face. He was doing this to her. The shadows under her eyes seemed to darken each time he spoke.

"King won't have to stay in bed." He hoped what the doctor told him would reassure Ellie better than it had him. "He can use a wheelchair. They'll deliver that this afternoon, too."

"A wheelchair!" Michael popped back up from the floor. "Wow, do you think King will let us ride in it? Mom, can we have races with our skateboards?"

Mitch shoved his fingers into his jeans pockets to keep from tousling Michael's hair again. Ellie made it pretty clear she didn't want him warming up to her kids. Good sense told him he shouldn't be wondering if her hair felt as soft as Michael's. Unfortunately good sense had never been his long suit.

Ellie rested her hands on her bouncing son's shoulders and shook her head.

"Aw, Mom, why not? I *want*—"

"A wheelchair isn't for racing, Michael." Mitch regretted the words the minute they were out of his mouth. He sounded positively *parental*.

Gabe frowned at him over the edge of his book. "They race them in the Special Olympics," he challenged.

"Hey, you're right." Since when had Mitch started acting like his old man? Since when did he think Ellie needed help with her own kids?

Ellie sighed. "Points for you, Gabe." She marked the air with two fingers, then kissed the end of one and touched it to Michael's nose. "But no rides for you, young man."

"Aw, Mom." Michael slumped to the floor.

Mitch shrugged off the thought of renting a second wheelchair just for the kids. A crazy attempt to win points for himself? A kiss from Ellie's fingertip? Damn, he was letting himself get way too involved here. And he hadn't told them the worst yet.

"King won't be running any races. You'll have to move him real slow—" he took a deep breath "—'cause his legs'll be sticking straight out in front of the chair."

"He'll run into the walls," Gabe announced tersely.

Mitch groaned as he watched Ellie's eyes widen in alarm. Out of the mouths of preadolescents—was that the saying?

"Things will go just fine, Gabe." Mitch doubted Gabe believed that any better than *he* did. "Your mom will be in charge of wheeling him around, and you guys will be in charge of keeping your toys out of the way. You can all help swing him in and out of bed while he pulls himself up on the trapeze. I'll put one in the bathroom, too, so—"

Gabe sat up and squinted at Mitch. "Who'll do all that stuff while we're in school?"

"School?" School wasn't out yet—Mitch knew that. Skiing vacations had long since passed, and families hadn't started showing up at Winterhaven for summer vacations. Jack always claimed this was Mitch's favorite time of the year—no kids, no lessons, no avalanches, no rescues.

"Mommy and I go to school, too," Seri piped up. "She's going to be a dentist."

"Seri..." Ellie shook her head at her daughter.

"You go to *school?*"

She nodded. "But my finals are done in two weeks. I'll be here after that."

"And she helps King in the store," Gabe added defiantly. "Are you going to help in the store now, too?"

Mitch couldn't believe it. "You go to school and you work in the store *and* you're trying to raise four kids?

Just how, exactly, were you planning to take care of King? Or maybe I should be asking *when?*''

His anger flared—at this too slender, too tired, too enticing little woman—for taking on more than any sane person could possibly handle; and at her defensive, protective son—for challenging Mitch's intentions. Most of all, he was angry at himself. For caring.

This wasn't like him. He never let himself get involved. Any more than it was like his father to get involved. The father he remembered never would have taken people into his home. And not just any people—a woman with four kids. And a *dog*. What had happened to his father?

What was happening to *him?*

He glared at Ellie, saw her pull herself up the way she did, like a little bird puffing her feathers to look bigger. But her blue, blue eyes didn't snap with electricity. She looked worried and tired. And he knew if she were in his arms, the top of her head would barely brush his chin.

Thoughts like that would get him into a whole lot of trouble. He fought to keep from reaching out to brush wisps of hair from her forehead. Undaunted, she turned her face up to him—and wiped out his resistance.

"I didn't know King would be so...restricted, but I'm sure he'll want to wheel himself around as soon as he can. When classes start again, I'll fix his lunch before I leave. The kids will be here after school."

She smiled up at Mitch, a tired, unwavering little smile that never made it to her eyes. "You don't need to worry about King. We'll manage, won't we, guys?"

Mitch wanted to yell at her. He wanted to believe her. Damn it, what he really wanted to do was kiss her. But he couldn't do any of those things.

"Ellie, you can't even lift the TV with the help of your ragtag kids. How do you think you can take care of King?"

Ellie's determined voice never faltered. "I always take care of my responsibilities."

In her eyes, he read the challenge, *What about you?*

Michael hopped from one foot to the other in front of the living-room windows. "When will they get here, Mom?"

"I don't know, hon. Why don't you go do something? Time will go by faster."

Following her own advice, Ellie moved from the windows that looked out on the tree-lined side street of KirkKnoll. Shoving hands deep into the pockets of her overalls, she circled the small living room for the fifth time, nudging Gabe's feet from the sofa where he'd stretched out to read a book. Feeling confined, she pulled her hands free, straightened magazines on the coffee table, picked up a stray crayon, combed fingers back through Rafe's hair. Bubba Sue looked up at her from her place next to him on the floor.

"How many more minutes?" Rafe never took his eyes from the cartoons on the reinstalled TV. Bubba Sue's tail thumped.

"I'm sure they'll be here soon."

But not soon enough. Ellie wanted to see King with her own eyes. She wanted to know for certain he was recovering from the terrible car crash. She wanted to evaluate for herself how difficult it would be to care for him.

"Mommy, how many minutes is soon?" Seri still perched on the windowsill, her nose pressed against the glass, a tissue-paper flower clutched in her hand.

Ellie glanced at her watch. "Maybe fifteen."

Fifteen minutes and Mitch and his father would be here. Half a day and Mitch would be gone. Just as she had hoped.

Be careful what you wish for. She could still hear her father's voice issuing his favorite warning. At eighteen, she'd wished for an exciting life, and look what Peter had given her. She glanced at her four beautiful children—all of whom Peter had abandoned.

When she and Peter had eloped, her father had disowned her. But he couldn't fault her wish this time. Mitch Kole was just another variation on her flamboyant ex-husband—full of charm and persuasion. But when responsibilities became too demanding, ready to head for the hills. In Mitch's case, the mountains. Hardly a fairytale kind of guy.

Ellie sighed. Mitch was far too attractive, but maybe she was finally beginning to learn that princes and rescues and the power of love only showed up in stories. Maybe she could start to trust her judgment again.

"They're here! I see Mitch's car! The King and The Prince are here!" Seri shouted. Bubba Sue started barking.

Michael grabbed a tissue flower from the sofa and thundered down the front stairs.

Seri tugged Ellie's hand. "Let's *go*, Mommy."

"We'll all go, but wait for me at the bottom."

That was all they needed. Flowers in hand, Rafe and Seri raced after Michael, the little black dog close behind. Only Gabe stalled at the top landing.

Ellie followed his gaze to the strange contraption in the ceiling of the stairwell that Mitch had rigged before breakfast. With a man like Mitch, there was always something new like this, something intriguing.

She waited as Gabe shuffled down the stairs behind her. At the bottom, he slouched against the door frame and dug his hands deep into his pockets.

"Okay, remember what I told you." Ellie directed her words especially to Michael. "Mitch is responsible for getting King upstairs. We'll help when it's needed. Otherwise, we'll stay out of the way."

That was what she'd decided last night. She would make sure Mitch got King safely settled in. She would have him show them how to take care of his father. Then they would all wave as he drove off to the airport.

She and her kids *would* manage. They had to. Somehow.

"They're here, they're here, can we go out now?" Michael pranced in the narrow entryway like a colt ready to run.

"Okay, but be care—" Before she could finish, they were out the door. All except Gabe. Just as well. The three younger ones were as excited and noisy as a circus parade—just the kind of welcome King needed to lift his spirits.

"Come on, sweetheart, let's go help." She put her arm around Gabe's shoulder and nudged him outside. "King will want to hear what you've been doing at the store."

She followed her children to the curb where King sat in the back seat of Mitch's rental car. They crowded around the older man delivering their paper flowers, but Ellie still managed to get a good look.

King looked better than she'd expected. For some reason, she'd imagined he would lose his salt-and-pepper hair. She'd worried that his broad shoulders would stoop and the mellow lines of his face would be tight with pain. It struck her again how much he looked like Mitch.

How much Mitch would someday look like him. But appearance was where the similarities ended, she thought with regret.

She moved nearer, and King smiled at her through the open car door, a warm, accepting smile, the kind her father had so rarely given her.

Abruptly his face knotted into an exaggerated scowl. "Rafe, come get this plastic bag out of here. It's got my toothbrush in it. And my bedpan." He winked broadly. "Gabe, Michael, get these sweet smellin' flowers away from me and give them to your mom before the darn things die. Here, Seri, you'll have to take care of this for me. Those nurses accused me of just keepin' on going." He handed her a giant pink rabbit with sunglasses, flip-flops and a big bass drum.

Seri squealed with delight. The stuffed animal was almost as big as she was.

"Where's that son of mine? Let's get this show on the road."

A muffled grunt rose from the rear of the car—the sound of a man about to lose his temper. Ellie resisted the urge to go to his rescue. Brief though the activity was, bringing King home was the one responsibility Mitch had accepted. She'd vowed to leave this much to him.

Another grunt followed, this one suspiciously like a word she didn't allow her children to hear. Good sense told her to keep her distance. Habit sent her hurrying to the car.

Mitch leaned almost double into the small trunk, tugging on a wheelchair. Reaching in, she straightened one of the smaller wheels. The chair pulled free. Mitch jerked backward.

"Ouch!" He dumped the chair on the pavement and reached up to rub his head. "Son of a—"

Ellie raised her eyebrows.

"...sea lion," he added lamely. "Darn small trunk," he muttered, working his fingers on his scalp.

Ellie shoved her hands into her pockets, which didn't help at all. She still had the urge to run her own fingers into his dark hair.

"Thanks," he grumbled. "I can take it from here." He opened the chair and wheeled it to the sidewalk.

She could see him measuring the distance to the front door, weighing the problem of getting King upstairs. As far as she could see, there was only one solution. King would just have to live in the car till he got his casts off.

But this wasn't her problem. This much Mitch had claimed as his own. She stepped back to watch.

"Okay, King, I have to lift you out."

Just as quickly, she rushed back across the sidewalk. "Mitch, you can't do that. He's too—" But he'd already reached inside the car.

Omigod. He hadn't set the wheelchair brakes.

She spun around, pressed both levers and flipped the foot rests into place. By the time she turned back, Mitch had King in his arms. She reached to guide King's legs out of the car.

That was when she saw what Mitch had told them yesterday. One of King's legs sported a plastic-type cast from his toes to his knee. The other leg stuck straight out in front of him with a cast that ran all the way from his foot to his hip. She felt herself getting light-headed.

"Ellie...there's a lever on the side...to extend the leg rest. Can you find it?" Mitch's breathing came heavy.

She whirled back to the wheelchair, searching franti-

cally for the leg extension. "I found it. It's up. Hurry."
Aching to help, she turned back, longing to soothe King,
to give Mitch more strength.

King patted Mitch on the shoulder. "Tables have
turned, haven't they, son? Used to be I carried you
around." He drew in a sharp breath. "Diaper didn't
weigh half as much as these damn things, though." He
scowled down at his casts.

Ellie saw Mitch's face freeze, felt tension spark the
air again. She'd sensed it before. What was there between father and son that caused Mitch such anger? Resentment seemed to roll off him like sweat. What made
him call his own father King?

Mitch lowered King carefully into the wheelchair, and
Ellie guided his legs into place. Then she made the mistake of looking up at the older man. His face had gone
taut. His swarthy coloring had turned chalk white. Moisture beaded above his lips.

Her heart clenched. "Are you all right?"

"Couldn't be better." He managed a labored grin as
he blotted a jacket sleeve against his forehead. "Okay,
kids, pretend I fell down a mountain. Mitch is going to
rescue me."

Ellie put her hand on King's arm. "This isn't a game.
I think we should call the hospital for help."

King patted her hand. "Mitch knows what he's doing,
Ellie. He's a member of Mountain Rescue. Don't worry,
a pair of Fiberglas long johns isn't going to keep me
down. Besides, I've always wanted to see what this boy
does in his spare time." He grinned up at Mitch. "What
say we get this over with, son?"

King might have thought he'd convinced her with his
bravado, but she saw his strain. Mitch might be more

than a ski instructor, but right now he looked as grim as an undertaker. She didn't feel good about this at all.

But there wasn't much she could do except help. She ran to hold the door while Mitch backed King up the step and into the entryway.

"Seri, Rafe, Michael—upstairs," Mitch commanded. "Remember how we practiced? Wheel that new chair into the living room and be ready when I call you."

They nodded solemnly, then raced up the stairs, Seri dragging the big pink rabbit, Bubba Sue barking the whole way.

"Gabe, I want you here to help your mom and me."

Any other man, Ellie would have refused to let command her children this way. But Mitch seemed to know what he was doing. She trusted him on this. The realization startled her.

Mitch unhitched the ropes he'd tied to the stair railing earlier that morning. Slowly they played through his hands, sliding upward through the three pulleys he'd attached at the top of the stairwell. A bunch of orange nylon straps descended to their level.

"This is the seat harness I told you about, King. It'll let us hoist you to the top."

Gabe stepped back. "No way!"

"Gabe?" Ellie felt the same fear she saw in her son's eyes, but she couldn't let him know.

"He can't do that, Mom. He'll hurt King. I won't—"

"We can do this, Gabe. I'm counting on your help." Mitch put his hand on Gabe's shoulder.

Ellie could almost feel the touch.

Gabe jerked free. "I'm just a kid. I can't do that."

Mitch hesitated. "You watch that rescue show on TV, don't you? Remember what I showed you? Kids can do a lot...when they *know* what to do."

Ellie sensed the tension emanating from Mitch, as if his words were directed at himself.

"It's okay to be scared, Gabe. You'll do a better job. I need you to guide King's legs while your mom and I hoist him up. I know you can do that. I just need to know if you will."

Gabe glared at Mitch, then turned away.

"Come on, Gabe," King coaxed. "Mitch *needs* your help. Operation Beanstalk—get the giant back up to the top."

Ellie held her breath. Something told her not to interfere. There were times when a mother's love wasn't enough for a boy to take that step, times when a son wouldn't ask, "Mother, may I." Too many times when a boy needed a father. It worried her so that Gabe didn't have one anymore.

Slowly Gabe turned back, his chin high, his mouth pressed in a grim line. "Okay. I'll do it."

King punched him on the shoulder. "That's my main man. Let's get movin'."

Suddenly things were happening too fast. Ellie couldn't keep track of the straps Mitch wove around King's legs and torso, nor the way he snapped and clipped and checked things into place. She wanted to test each connection, to hug Gabe, to pat King reassuringly on the back. When Mitch bounded up the stairs without another word, she wanted to call him back.

But she didn't. Reluctantly she climbed the stairs after him, loath to leave her son and King alone at the bottom. They looked so vulnerable, but soothing hands weren't what they needed now. They needed strength. Mitch needed whatever strength she had to offer upstairs with him.

At the top, she stood where Mitch pointed and held

the ropes the way he'd shown her. Her heart raced with
fear. What if together they weren't strong enough? What
if Gabe couldn't guide King's legs? What if the ropes
slipped?

"You ready, King?"

"Ready when you are, son."

"Then up you come."

The pulleys squealed, and Ellie's heart lurched. Mitch
pulled, hand over hand, feeding the ropes to her. Bracing
herself against the stair railing, she held them taut, guid-
ing them to coil safely at the side. Her pulse thundered.

Mitch's shoulders stretched and knotted under his in-
digo sweatshirt. Circles of darker blue appeared under
his arms and down the middle of his back. Heat radiated
from him—and the earthy scent of a man working.

How could she notice such things at a time like this?

How could she not?

Together, Mitch and she tugged King slowly up the
stairwell. King clutched the ropes of his harness like the
tethers of a swing. Below him Gabe held his legs firmly
away from the walls.

"Fee, fie, foe, fum, I smell the blood of children,"
King chanted. "And when I get to the top, I'm going to
eat them all."

Behind her, Ellie heard her children giggle. The dog's
tail thumped the floor.

"Hey, guys," Mitch called. "Ready with that wheelchair?"

As King reached the landing, the children rolled the
chair into place and set the brake. Carefully Mitch
guided his father above the seat.

"Okay, King, down you go."

Like a space shuttle docking with the main ship, King

settled in, one leg stretched out on the leg extension, the other square on the footrest.

King let out an audible breath. "Just wheel me away from those stairs, Ellie. Thank goodness I don't have to face that trip again for a while."

How long was a while? And when it was up, how were she and the kids ever going to get King back down? She glanced at Mitch, but he was busy slipping clips and straps from around King's body.

"When do you have to go back to the doctor?"

"Not for a month." King sounded relieved.

Seri danced in front of him. "We can play Rapunzel!"

A whole month. "Good. By then I'll find someone to help us get you back down."

"Not to worry. Mitch will be here."

The pride in King's face made Ellie's heart hurt. Why hadn't Mitch told him he wouldn't be staying? Silly question. She glanced at Mitch again, but he'd moved to the stair railing to anchor the ropes. He was avoiding the whole scene.

Fine. She could handle this, even if Mitch couldn't. "King, I told Mitch to go back to Colorado. He has...things he has to do. The kids and I can take care of you."

"Now, Ellie, I know you think you owe me, but you've more than earned your place here. Mitch will take care of me. He told me this morning he'll stay long enough to take me back to the doctor in a month. There's another bed coming this afternoon so he'll be near when I need him at night."

"Hooray! Mitch can play Rapunzel, too!" Seri danced around Mitch where he knelt on the landing.

When he didn't look up, she put her little hand on his cheek. "*Will* you play with me?" she asked wistfully.

Ellie thought her heart would break. *Please tell her no*, she silently prayed. *Tell her you're not staying—not for a whole month.*

Mitch looked up at Ellie. His jaw knotted, and his eyes darkened with the same tension she'd seen before. He held her gaze for what seemed like minutes, long enough to send unwanted anticipation skittering through her. Then he turned back to her daughter.

"Sure, kid, I'll play. But you'll have to teach me how."

Chapter Three

Mitch watched Ellie pick at her food. Stubborn woman. She was so busy looking after everyone else, she wasn't taking care of herself. Somebody ought to give her a lecture.

Without looking up, Ellie gathered her still half-filled plate and an empty casserole dish and disappeared into the kitchen.

Mitch looked at the kids expectantly. Nobody moved. He drummed his fingers on the table, then grabbed up his own dishes and another serving bowl and followed Ellie to the kitchen. She'd been avoiding him all afternoon; she'd refused his help on everything except getting King settled. But she wasn't going to avoid him now.

Still, he had to admit, she was a whole lot smarter than he. At least she was trying to keep some distance between them. Spending a month looking after his father was onerous enough, but with Ellie here, he'd be smart to hole up in the opposite end of the flat. Shoot, he'd be better off on the opposite side of the moon. Unfortunately he couldn't seem to muster even the slightest effort to stay away from her. He didn't *want* to stay away from her.

She passed him on her return from the kitchen, walking a wide berth around him. "Finish your pudding, everyone. Put those plates down, Mitch. The kids take care of the dishes."

Ignoring her orders, he balanced more dirty plates hazardously up his arm and carried them to the kitchen. "I'm doing dishes tonight," he called back. "The kids can spend time with King. You can study."

"Yeah!" Michael shouted. Bubba Sue barked.

Mitch returned just in time to see Michael jump from his chair and dash to the TV.

"We can watch cartoons. Do you want to, King? Which one do you want to see first?"

"Michael, sit down," Ellie chided. "You can decide after we clean up."

"*Mo*-om!" The chorus from the table was unanimous. Even Rafe spoke up, and Gabe forgot to look rebellious. Bubba Sue barked her vote.

Mitch read Ellie's objections in her eyes—along with reluctant defeat. She was completely outnumbered. But she drew in a deep breath and raised her chin a good queenly inch.

"Okay, I'll do KP this time. I'm sure your father would like your company, too, Mitch." She refused to look at him.

Oh, but she was unyielding, this proud little woman. So unwilling to accept help. Except from King, Mitch reminded himself.

He cast an uncomfortable glance at his father. To his relief, King seemed absorbed in folding a napkin.

"I'm doing the dishes, Ellie. King and I will be to-gether plenty while you're all in school." He and his father would have more than enough time, Mitch brooded, more than he'd planned to spend here ever again. He wasn't sure why he'd decided to stay, but before he dealt with that question, he had another prob-lem to resolve. As usual, it was himself.

He had to find a way to put Ellie into perspective. Which was another way of saying *get her out of his mind.* He'd *never* been attracted to homey-type women. The females he spent time with at Winterhaven probably used pudding as a facial pack. He doubted any of them ever dipped their fancy French manicures into something as mundane as a kitchen sink. They weren't interested in commitments. That worked just fine for him.

A heaping dose of domesticity—that was all he needed. An extended session of playing house with the single mom of four daddy-starved kids—that should be enough to cool any red-blooded American male's jets.

"Okay, guys, check the floor for obstacles, 'cause Old King Kole is on the move," Mitch drawled.

King pushed his wheelchair away from the table. "Thanks for the great meal, Ellie. Hospital food was like fried floor mops and gooey glue drops." He winked at Seri.

"*Eeyuuuww.*" Seri made a face. The boys broke up laughing. The little black terrier yipped.

Mitch caught himself smiling. He'd forgotten King's off-the-wall humor—and the way he used to thank Mitch's mother for dinner the rare times he'd eaten at home. *The food on the circuit tastes like chopped floor mats and boiled vampire bats,* he might say. They'd laughed a lot at meal times. Mitch had forgotten.

"Okay," Ellie commanded. "Everyone help Mitch

move King. Then back to clear the table.'' She glared at Mitch, her blue eyes flashing with challenge.

He didn't dare overrule her on that. Instead he arranged King in front of the TV, then helped the kids finish the table. When Ellie brought King's coffee and medications, Mitch fought the temptation to stick around, to watch her administer her gentle care. *Not smart,* he scolded himself. Time to retreat to the kitchen.

The sight made him groan. Pots and pans lay everywhere. Dishes leaned in precarious piles on the counters and balanced on the breakfast bar. Ellie must have tried to include all the dietary requirements the doctor had prescribed for King in one meal. That meant a lot of dishes in the next month!

Well, he'd asked for it. *Domesticity, here I come.*

Shoving up his shirtsleeves, he opened the dishwasher. Empty, of course. Ellie was the kind of woman who never left a job undone. *A tough act to follow, Kole.* But he wasn't going for a Martha Stewart award. All he wanted was Ellie—out of his mind. Out of his fantasies. He grabbed the nearest plates and slid them into the dishwasher.

''Just like a man.''

She stood framed in the doorway, her shoulder propped against the white woodwork. Her shapeless navy cardigan hung to her knees, and her faded overalls made her look more like a kid than a grown woman.

Something twisted inside him that felt suspiciously like protectiveness. She was so damn small. So vulnerable. Too young to be the mother of four kids.

She also looked amused…and downright delicious.

He turned back to the sink before his thoughts got the better of him. ''Being a man, I tend to operate like one, Ellie. Whatever I'm doing wrong, I suggest you not look a gift horse in the mouth. You're supposed to be studying.'' He slipped more dishes into the bottom dividers, resisting the urge to turn and do more than just look at her.

"If I leave you to finish, we won't have dishes tomorrow."

"I know, I know, my mother used to say they had to be rinsed first, but dishwashers were made to—"

"It doesn't work."

"It *does*. I *never* used to rinse—"

"I mean the dishwasher. It's broken." She grinned. "You'll have to do them by hand."

"Oh." *Tantalizing mouth. What would it be like to kiss those full pink lips?* Quickly he stooped and opened the cupboard to search for soap.

"It's right there on the counter."

Before he could stand, she crossed to the sink. Her sweater brushed his shoulder as she leaned around him, and he remembered the way she'd brushed by him in the hall, remembered his reaction—could it have been only yesterday?

Gripping the cupboard handle, he made himself crouch where he was. Because he knew if he stood, she'd be right in front of him, and the feathery dark gold of her hair would barely brush his chin. He knew if she raised her face, he would have to kiss her.

"Why don't you go watch TV with your father?" she commanded. "I can get these done in a hurry."

"Why don't you go study for your finals? I can wash dishes fast, too." Somehow he managed to stand and move out of kissing range all in one motion, though when he looked at her, he couldn't remember why he'd wanted to. She was studying him curiously, and the curve of her mouth threatened to give in to another grin.

"I had no idea you were a man of so many talents."

"I fix dishwashers, too." Hell, he was acting like a kid bucking for teacher's approval.

She reached for the faucets, ran water into the sink, added a swirl of green soap. She was avoiding him again.

Avoidance is good, he told himself. This homey little scenario was supposed to be neutralizing her effect on him, not getting him more involved.

"Okay, Ellie, how about a compromise. We clean up together, then you study and I fix the dishwasher. That way we won't have to fight over dishes anymore."

From a drawer, she retrieved a towel and shoved it at him. "Okay. I wash, you dry. First, bring me the dishes."

"Right." He started with the breakfast bar, working his way nearer until he had nothing to do except stand beside her and dry things as she balanced them in the drain rack. Which put him far too near. Yet not nearly close enough.

He shuffled a bit closer, watching the way her silky hair swayed against her shoulders, hiding her face, then falling back to expose the delicate line of her chin. A little closer and he could catch that clean scent of—

She shifted a full step to the left. "You're a pretty good dish wiper. For a guy."

He almost dropped a bowl, but he didn't yield an inch.

At arm's length, she held out a dripping plate, forcing him back. "When we were growing up, my sister used to dry."

He took the dish, closing the gap as she turned back to the sink. "You didn't have a dishwasher? Where'd you live?"

She glanced at him with amusement. "Not in the

backwoods, if that's what you mean. We lived here…in KirkKnoll. Over in Adams Orchard. We did have a dishwasher…*and* indoor plumbing.'' There was that wry humor in her eyes as she shoved another plate at him.

Adams Orchard. Custom-built houses on big, wooded lots. Money. If Ellie came from a home like that, why was she here?

''My mother wouldn't do her china and silverware in the dishwasher. She was of the opinion that the family who does housework together stays together, so we washed and dried every night. We did most everything around the house.''

''What's your father do?''

''Stockbroker. Mom's a librarian. After my sister and I left home, they moved to New York so my father could try his hand on Wall Street.''

So Ellie had grown up with money. A mother who insisted on togetherness and a father who stayed around, at least till his kids were grown. The kind of family Mitch had never known. The kind of family Ellie still wanted, no doubt. Another reason to put about a million miles between them—instead of trying to break through her defenses.

He set the plates into the cupboard and turned back for another. ''You see your folks often?''

She swished a plate under hot water. Set it in the drainer. ''I haven't seen them in eleven years,'' she answered quietly.

''Eleven *years?*'' Surely he'd misunderstood.

''Yep.''

She'd probably aimed for nonchalance, but her valiant attempt hit him hard. ''Ellie, why?''

For a long moment she kept her face averted.

Impulsively Mitch stepped closer, slipped a knuckle

under her chin and nudged her gently to look at him.
Her eyes glittered blue...and sad. Moisture pooled at the
rims. A tear broke loose to slip down her cheek.

How could something so small be so painful to watch?
"Ellie, I'm sorry. I didn't mean to..." Slowly he
brushed the heel of his thumb across her smooth skin,
trying to wipe away her sadness. He felt a tremor run
through her.

"Ellie, why? What happened?" he murmured. He
couldn't bear to see her so unhappy. He leaned nearer.
"Ellie?"

She raised her face slowly, her eyes full of reluctance
and uncertainty...and desire?

Whatever it was, it was his undoing. Gently he closed
his mouth over hers. She hesitated, as if she weren't sure
what to do. Then her lips softened, her body yielded, her
head tilted until her mouth found the shape of his. She
tasted warm and sweet.

Heat shafted through him, and he felt himself respond.
She was so small, so soft, so lush under his hands. So
sweetly shy. Never before had he wanted to kiss a
woman so badly, so gently, at the same time he wanted
to—

"Are you guys going to kiss for a long time?"

Ellie went stiff in his arms. "Seri!" she whispered.
Spinning away, she plunged her hands into the dishwater
and began scrubbing.

Leaving Mitch to stare down at a big-eyed little urchin
who waited for an answer.

"Well, Princess..." He wrestled with several possible
prevarications, stalling, trying to cool down. Finally he
just gave up. "As a matter of fact, I think we were. But
the clock just struck twelve."

For what seemed like a hundred years, Seri regarded

him with those serious brown eyes. Then she smiled. "Okay. If you're not going to kiss any more right now, would you please come read me a story?"

Behind him, Mitch heard a strangled cough. "Yes, sweetheart, Mitch would *love* to read you a story, wouldn't you, Mitch?"

"But the dishes—"

"I'm almost finished. Please, just go."

He didn't want to. He didn't want to stop kissing her, even though it left him completely out of control. But for once, he needed to do something besides what he wanted.

"Okay, Ellie." He backed reluctantly toward the door. "But I'll be back."

"*No!* I mean, I don't need any more help."

"What about fixing the dishwasher?"

"Oh." She hesitated. "On one condition." Her tone had become firm and determined again.

"Which is?"

"After you're done working on it, you pay the repair bill."

Why hadn't she stopped him? Mindlessly Ellie swished and scrubbed, sprayed and stacked—because that one question overwhelmed her. *Why?*

She'd let Mitch kiss her; she'd *wanted* him to. Her promise to stay away from him had flown away like so much fairy dust when he'd looked down at her with such concern.

She'd wanted to kiss *him*. She had no business wanting to kiss any man, much less Mitch. Mitch wasn't the staying-around kind.

But he *was* staying around—for a whole month; there was no getting out of that. She couldn't even try to persuade him to leave because they needed him. He'd proven it today with all he'd done to help with King.

But she and her kids had to stay, too. Even if she could find a cheap apartment and another job, King needed *them*. She was convinced of that. Alone, Mitch and whoever he might hire wouldn't give King healing love. He needed that more than anything right now.

She had to find a way to keep Mitch out of her life. Out of her children's lives. Out of all their hearts.

Swiping the countertops one last time, she stopped stalling and marched into the main room to clean the table. Head down, she tried to ignore the crew planted in front of the TV. In spite of herself, she peeked.

Rafe was stretched out on his stomach beside King's wheelchair with the dog nestled under one hand and the portable phone in the other. Gabe occupied his usual spot on the plaid couch—his shoes off for once, she was glad to see. Michael curled in the old black beanbag on King's other side, shifting and wiggling like a bucket of worms.

Seri and Mitch weren't there.

It was her own fault. She never would have sent them off together if she hadn't been so…distracted. If she hadn't needed to be away from Mitch.

With determination, she marched down the hall to King's bedroom. Mitch had insisted she and Seri move in there to sleep. It still vexed her that he thought the boys would be better help with King during the night than she.

Through the doorway, Seri's night-light revealed only King's smoothly made, four-poster bed, just as he'd left it before his accident. Except that an old stuffed tiger and a worn teddy bear had taken up residence on the pillows.

Ellie retraced her steps, striding through the kitchen and into the second flat.

"And you're supposed to talk real slow."

Seri's voice told Ellie she'd found them this time. She stopped in the doorway to the Mermaid Room.

"Okay. What else should I know?"

Mitch sounded terribly serious, as if he were giving Seri his undivided attention. In all her four years, Seri had rarely enjoyed that kind of attention from her daddy. Except when it came to The Angels, Ellie thought bitterly.

"When it's the girl's turn, you talk like a girl, and when it's the boy's—well, you know how to talk." Seri giggled.

Ellie peered into the dusky room, lit only by a small study lamp on the scarred old desk. The mermaid comforter lay kind of crooked across the bed. Army figures rested on each of the pillows.

In spite of herself, Ellie smiled. Seri was too young to be making beds, but she did her best. She'd even tried to make mermaids more tolerable to Michael and Rafe now that they'd be sleeping in here.

"Okay, I think I've got it."

Ellie's gaze moved to Seri where she sat cross-legged on the floor between Mitch and the big pink rabbit. They all faced the windows—as if they'd been looking out at the stars. Making wishes, maybe? The thought wrenched Ellie's heart. Seri needed this kind of attention, but not from this kind of man.

"Shall *I* tell it to *you* this time?" Mitch asked.

"Yes." A contented little sigh. "Please."

Ellie knew she should interrupt. She should stop this now, before—

"Okay, Princess. Once upon a time...in a faraway land...a long time ago..."

Still, he followed Seri's instructions pretty well.

"...a man and a woman had a beautiful little baby girl."

Not bad for a ski instructor. He said the words slowly, using his deep "boy's" voice, just as Seri had told him.

"Not man and woman, silly. King and Queen."

Ellie's smile faded. This sounded suspiciously like the kind of story that also involved a prince. A Prince Charming.

"Oops. Sorry. So this *King* and *Queen* had a baby, see."

A knot of disapproval tightened in Ellie's chest. The kind of story that promised unrealistic expectations of love for imaginative little girls.

"And they named her Seraphina."

Seri giggled.

"No," Ellie whispered.

"Now, let's see if I can remember. The King and Queen gave this big party, see, so all the local fairies could come and give Seraphina toys and dolls and chocolate and stuff. All the fairies except numero thirteen, because they had this problem about only twelve plates, so—"

"No!" Ellie rushed into the room. "Stop right there."

"Mommy, Mitch is telling me *Sleeping Beauty*."

"No, he's not. You know the rules. No fairy tales!" Then she made the mistake of looking more closely at the two of them. Seri's dark eyes filled with tears. Mitch's frown grew grimmer by the second.

How could she do this to her daughter?

Because it was for her own good. No stories of young

girls being rescued by unrealistic heroes. Young girls should learn to take care of themselves.

"Seri, I want you to go—" Ellie stopped. She couldn't do it. She was asking too much of her little girl. How could she expect a four-year-old to understand her mother's second rule? *No more fly-by-night men.*

A mouse story, that was what they needed. Surely Mitch couldn't capture Seri's heart with a rodent—even if it was cute and precocious. She searched through the dog-eared books between the metal bookends on the desk.

"Here." She slapped the book into Mitch's hands. "Mice are good. Do this one. Then it's time for bed. And remember—" she raised a finger, aimed it at him *"—no more fairy tales!"*

She whirled and fled from the room.

Ellie flipped on the small light above the breakfast counter and slapped her notebook down.

A pen. She'd need a pen. Kneeling, she dug one out of the hand-me-down backpack Rafe had rejected last fall. He was a first-grader now, he'd said, too grown-up for genies and magic lamps. She'd been so proud of him. Even if the cost of another book bag had come hard.

She sighed. Climbed onto the stool. If only she could trust that *she'd* finally grown up. The way she acted around Mitch wasn't very encouraging.

Pushing him from her mind, she settled onto the stool and opened her notes. *Anatomy and Physiology II.*

What she really needed was an intensive course on the anatomy and physiology of the human heart. Ignoring the thought, she read through the first paragraph.

How was she going to protect her children from Mitch when he was so...charming? So intriguing. So...likable.

She read the paragraph again.

Who was she kidding? Gabe back-talked Mitch on almost every word, and Rafe was so busy waiting for a call from his father, he hardly knew Mitch was there. As for Michael, nowadays he seemed to latch on to *any* man within hearing distance.

It was Seri she worried about.

Darn! She read the paragraph a third time, but the words passed before her eyes like hieroglyphics.

Closing the notebook, she propped her chin in her palms and remembered her daughter's tears. Darn it, sometimes being a parent meant teaching things that didn't promise happy endings. Sometimes it meant making rules that hurt.

From across the counter, she plucked a pale pink tissue from a box. Rules such as not trusting men with laughter in their eyes. Absently she folded the tissue in half, pleated it accordion style and wrapped a yellow twisty around the middle. Rules such as not believing men with false promises in their voices.

Her fingers worked automatically, tearing away bits from the ends of the folded tissue, making them uneven and feathery. Carefully, she separated the layers into ruffled petals.

She didn't want to hurt Seri or the boys—ever. But they had to grow up knowing that in real life happily-ever-after wasn't guaranteed. Fairy tales really didn't come true.

She fluffed the flower until it looked a bit like a carnation. Her rules might be harsh, but her children knew she loved them. They knew she would always be here for them.

Drawing a fortifying breath, she laid the flower on the counter. She would give it to Seri when she tucked her in. But before she kissed her daughter good-night, she would remind her that Mitch lived in Colorado. As soon as King got better, Mitch was going to leave. For good.

And while she was at it, Ellie would remind herself as well.

Dubiously she eyed the books on the counter. Not much chance she'd get any studying done now. Sliding from the stool, she retrieved the overflowing mending basket and her sewing kit from a lower cupboard. A familiar blue shirt lay on top, one sleeve all but amputated in a brotherly scuffle, though she couldn't remember which boy had been wearing it at the time. It looked too small for Gabe anymore.

She threaded a needle, found a thimble and climbed back into the comforting circle of light to stitch the shirt together.

"You're supposed to be studying, you know."

Ellie's heartbeat jumped. Mitch shouldn't startle her like that, showing up without making a sound.

She kept her eyes on her work. "Look, I apologize for making such a scene about the story."

"Guess every mother's entitled to a scene now and then."

She could feel him watching her. "I didn't used to be such a scold." Not that she cared what he thought.

"Before their father left?"

Her head snapped up. Had she told him that? With everything so unsettled, she couldn't remember what she'd said. She was too tired to try to remember.

Mitch meandered to the sink on the far side of the kitchen. "I can imagine you telling them fairy tales yourself once." Turning on the faucet, he filled the coffeepot. "With a librarian mother, I'll bet you know them all by heart."

He was right, of course, but his insight surprised her. What else would a librarian do but read to her daughters all the magical stories she loved?

"Not anymore." No room in her heart for stories now. No room for anything—or anyone—except her kids.

"King said your husband played the trumpet. King used to play himself, you know."

"Ex-husband," she stated sharply.

"Sorry." He sounded embarrassed. "Careless of me."

Surprised, she glanced up. In the dim light all she could see was his silhouette as he rummaged in a cupboard. He seemed so out of place here, like a football player at a tea party. Mitch belonged outdoors where he could burn off some of that...potency.

Quickly she looked back to her sewing, ignoring the heated memory of his kiss. She heard him scoop coffee grounds into the filter and return the can to the cupboard.

"Want to talk about it, Ellie?"

"No." She kept her eyes on her stitches, listened to the burble of the coffeemaker.

Maybe it was because Mitch stayed on the other side of the counter. Maybe it was because she felt safe in her small circle of light. Maybe it was because, in the year since Peter had walked out, Mitch was the only one to ask. But unexpectedly Ellie found herself talking.

"My mother and father were so different—Mom always telling us to try for our dreams, Dad monitoring our every move. I wanted to go away to college—anywhere to get away from his scrutiny. But he insisted I go to school here."

She breathed in the scent of brewing coffee and watched Mitch move around the edge of her light, fetching mugs from the cupboard. Separated from her by the breakfast counter.

"I met Peter that summer. Peter Angelo—that's what he called himself on stage. He was blond—what my friends called drop-dead gorgeous. My father called him 'silver-tongued and slippery.' Said he could charm a wasp's nest into submission." She stopped stitching.

Across the room, Mitch poured coffee into the mugs. He set them on the counter, leaning forward to slide hers over to her. He was watching her again.

Holding her breath, she tied a knot and cut the thread, ready to run if he came nearer. She didn't dare look up.

"So your mother overruled, and you were married in a big church in a big fancy wedding," he prompted, resting his elbows on the counter.

She tried to ignore him, flicking a finger through a box of buttons for a match to those on the shirt. "No." She took a deep, painful breath. "Peter talked me into eloping the week before I was supposed to start at Washington University."

A long silence. Then, "You must have fallen hard."

She glanced up. Mitch had retreated into the shadows, which accounted for why he sounded suddenly so distant.

"I fell for a fairy tale." There it was, the real reason she was telling him all this—so he'd know why fairy tales were forbidden to her children. "Except that Peter wasn't the pied piper after all, and we had to pawn the cow for beans. And we never owned even a shoe to live in."

"But you had The Angels."

Her head snapped up. "How did you—?" But of course, Seri had told him.

She didn't want to remember, didn't want to tell him

all this. But he needed to know why there was no place for a man in her life anymore.

"No angels at first—just one big adventure. No restrictions, no father to say no. Just traveling all over, staying out late, basking in Peter's applause."

She selected a button, began stitching it on the shirt. "Then I got pregnant. And it turned out Peter had just as many restrictions as my father. He didn't want a family. He didn't want to settle down. He wanted 'fame.' Kids were just baggage."

She ran a hand over the shirt, trying to smooth away the wrinkles. "When Gabe was born, for a while Peter seemed to change. He insisted on naming him, insisted he learn to play as soon as he was big enough to sit at a keyboard. Peter was that way with all the kids. The only time he spent with them was teaching them music. He even taught them to sing harmony."

She folded the shirt and laid it on the next stool, then reached into the mending basket for a pair of jeans. "We moved a lot. Fought a lot. I begged him to settle down, but every new gig was going to be his big breakthrough. He began leaving us behind, staying away longer."

Working the pull tab of the zipper, she tried to unsnag it from the jeans fabric. "A year ago he insisted we all go to Branson. He told me 'Peter Angelo and His Four Angels' were scheduled for an audition. Seri was barely three!"

She tugged fiercely on the jammed zipper of the jeans. "We had another fight. He took them to the audition anyhow." She jerked at the fabric, but the slider wouldn't budge. "They didn't make callbacks." Giving up, she let the pants drop to her lap, buried her hands in their soft warmth. "The next morning he was gone. So was our rattletrap van."

Mitch wandered around the end of the counter.

She stiffened, ready to get up and leave.

His face half in shadow, he hiked a hip onto a stool and sipped at his coffee. "And you couldn't call your parents because they'd disowned you."

Mitch didn't sound sarcastic, though she almost couldn't blame him if he were. Everything with Peter had been sort of melodramatic, and it was her own fault. She'd kept trying to believe he would change.

"Not exactly disowned. After we eloped, Dad…" Her voice caught. "My father didn't want to see me anymore. But my mother stayed in contact. She calls. We write. She sends money sometimes. Things for the kids. But I would *never* ask her to rescue us. I got myself into this." She gave the zipper another determined yank.

"Enter the King, stage left."

This time there was no mistaking the cynicism in Mitch's voice, though it wasn't directed at her. Something had come between Mitch and *his* father, too, a long time ago. Whatever it was, Mitch needed to get to know his father *now*.

He pushed off the stool, and her pulse kicked up a shaky notch. "Your father was in Branson for auditions, too—with a young band he'd been mentoring. We talked a little between performances."

He moved nearer, breaching her protective circle of light.

"But he didn't rescue us, Mitch." And she didn't feel protected anymore. She felt as if she were on the edge of a very tall building looking down. "He was a perfect gentleman."

Mitch reached for the jeans, brushed her fingers as he grasped them. She tried to hold on, tried not to look up at him. "He offered me a way to work things out... my...self."

He was standing too near. He was watching her too closely.

Slowly he slid the jeans from her hands. At last he turned his gaze to the zipper and she could start breathing again. Maybe he wasn't going to kiss her.

Mitch worked the fabric until it tugged free from the pull tab. "King always appreciated a pretty woman. You're a very pretty woman, Ellie." His dark eyes captured hers again, making her warm and wanting.

He laid the jeans on the counter. "You were right when you said only someone like me would think what I did about the two of you. I'm a lot like my father, Ellie. Neither of us has a very good record with commitments. But if I'd been in his shoes that day in Branson, I'd have offered whatever you'd asked to come live with me."

Dazed, she watched him lift her hand and gently remove the thimble. Holding her hand between them, he captured her gaze again and tugged her gently from the stool.

"I don't believe in fairy tales, either, Ellie. And I know the difference between a thimble and a kiss."

Chapter Four

Ellie could hardly breathe. The whole world seemed to hold its breath. The warmth of Mitch's hands radiated through her, glowed brighter. Every detail drifted into her awareness, moving her, awakening her. Mitch's touch, so gentle yet so enveloping, making her feel...cherished. Her own hand, reaching to reclaim her silvery thimble, to grasp at some sense of reality... And then his eyes, dark and deep, full of heat, flaming a need in her to touch him, too.

She knew better. She searched his face for that roguish grin that would stop her, but Mitch's eyes only reflected her own desire. In spite of everything, she raised her hand to his shirt, felt his heartbeat through her fingertips. Knew it throbbed in answer to her own trembling.

For she was trembling. Her veins ran with quicksilver as her fingers searched for the naked warmth of his neck, the tantalizing softness of his hair. He drew her against him, and her body quaked. He leaned down, and she rose on tiptoes to claim his kiss.

His mouth met hers, hard and seeking, shaping and reshaping to the hunger of her own lips. She opened to his gentle probing, and he tasted of coffee and sugar and an essence that could only be Mitch, all mountains and sunshine and heady musk.

This shouldn't be happening. She shouldn't be feeling what she was feeling. She wanted this man. Never in her life had she wanted a man this way.

Mitch encircled her waist, drawing her deeper into the kiss, making her aware of every inch of her body pressed against him. Every hard, burning surface of him. She couldn't get enough of him. Surely she would melt…or burn…or fly away in billows of smoke if he didn't—

Somewhere, from the far reaches of the universe, a faint *tink* sounded. Like a muted silver bell…that rang just once. Once almost wasn't enough.

With more resolve than she knew she possessed, she went still in his arms.

Mitch had dropped the thimble, the symbol of everything she'd become—the one person wholly responsible for her four wonderful children.

"Ellie?"

His lips near her ear sent tremors shimmering through her.

She pushed away, and he didn't try to hold her. Backing from his arms, she knelt to search the floor.

"I know the difference between a thimble… Here it is." She stood, pushing the thimble back onto her finger, holding her hand in front of her like a shield. "I know what a thimble is, too, Mitch. It's to protect against hurt."

"Ellie, I—"

"I'm going to put my children to bed now. Shouldn't you be taking care of your father?"

His questioning eyes darkened in frustration. "Ellie, don't—"

"This has nothing to do with fairy tales, Mitch, and we both know it. I think we need to get back to reality."

Snatching up the mended clothes, she rushed to find the safety of her children.

"Breakfast!" Mitch shoveled scrambled eggs onto the five plates spread out across the breakfast counter.

With his free hand, Rafe picked up a fork and poked at the yellow mound tentatively. His other hand clutched the portable phone.

Mitch flinched. From the look on the kid's face, he might as well have served him a dissected frog.

On the next stool, Seri polished off her fourth piece of bacon and licked her fingers clean.

At least Mitch had finally gotten that part right. The bacon had to be just so to please Her Highness.

"I don't want any breakfast," Gabe hollered down the hall.

Mitch gritted his teeth. It was the same argument every morning. He flung the kitchen towel over his shoulder. "You have to eat breakfast," he shouted. "Your brain needs food to learn." Grabbing a fork, he mashed tuna onto the four pieces of bread laid out on the counter.

"The eggs are gooey," Rafe complained. "And I don't like tuna."

"Rafe *always* wants peanut butter and jelly," Seri reminded Mitch.

"Peanut butter and jelly every day?" No wonder the kid hardly talked. His tongue was stuck to the roof of his mouth. Still mumbling, Mitch dug more bread from the wrapper.

Somewhere in the distance, the sound of running water stopped. "Mitch, is Michael up yet?"

At the sound of Ellie's voice, Mitch's bad temper threatened to cut loose. He could imagine her rushing from the shower, barely toweling off before throwing on one of those dismal long skirts and oversize sweaters that hid all her warm softness, whipping a comb through her silky hair and dashing from King's room to resolve half a dozen crises all at once.

For some reason, the whole scenario, from luscious bather to grunge supermom, just made him madder.

"Michael," he shouted. "Off your...bottom and on your feet. Bus in ten minutes." He dragged the peanut butter from the cupboard.

Mitch's imagination was working too damned well. So was his memory. He'd survived almost *two weeks* of domestic overdose, and he was still thinking about that evening in the kitchen. Still overheating every time he remembered Ellie's kiss and her hungry softness against him.

He still wanted her. In spite of all this reality.

He swiped a sleeve across his forehead. *If you can't stand the heat, get out of the kitchen, Kole.*

Gabe slouched to the counter, slid a piece of toast onto a paper napkin and scooped the eggs on top.

Mitch pretended not to notice.

"Faucet's dripping in the bathroom," Gabe challenged. "A lot." He ambled away, folded napkin in his hands.

First the dishwasher, then the bedroom light switch, now the faucets? The place was falling down around their ears. King had never been any good at fixing things.

"I'll take a look at it while King's with Mrs. Givens."

King was just one more thing that needed fixing. He wasn't doing well. Appetite was terrible. Every day he grew quieter. Damn it, he just didn't seem to be trying.

Mitch dragged in a deep breath. He hoped the visiting health aide would have some suggestions. Hiring no-nonsense Harriet Givens had probably been the most rational thing he'd done since he'd arrived.

"Mitch, better go roust Michael," Ellie called.

And staying here with a woman like Ellie had been the most— Damn, he had to stop thinking about her.

"Michael, get a move on!" he bellowed. Slathering jelly across a second slice of bread, he slapped the two together.

Ellie rushed into the kitchen. "Hey, guys, better get going."

At the sight of her, Mitch straightened abruptly. "Ouch! Gaw-l *darm*, that cupboard's hard." He rubbed his head, fighting the urge to punch the stupid cabinet.

Every day that went by she looked better to him. Tendrils of still-damp hair feathered around her face like wisps of butterscotch, and the dark circles under her blue eyes had diminished. She smelled fresh and cool, like some flowery soap. Even in her campy clothes, just the sight of her almost made him forget his bad mood.

It wasn't the cupboard that was stupid around here.

Ellie's gaze skittered away from him, as it did every time they were together. "Eat your eggs, Rafe. Seri, go get your stuff for day care. We leave in five minutes. Mitch, your father's still sleeping. I didn't have the heart to wake him. His pills are on the nightstand. Be sure he takes them."

She bit off a corner of toast. "Oh, and don't forget, three mothers are coming at ten to upgrade their kids' rental instruments." She glanced up at him. "At the store? You will remember to open the store, won't you?''

The store. Right. How could he forget? As soon as he renovated the entire plumbing system and did the week's laundry. How did she keep up with everything around here?

"I won't forget, Ellie." Especially when she looked so concerned. Especially when she looked so damned kissable.

"Good." Her gaze veered away as if she'd read his thoughts. "Michael," she called. "Are you—? Oh, dear."

Michael stood in the doorway rubbing his eyes and wearing a toothless grin. "I'm up, Mom." Beside him, Bubba Sue thumped her tail.

Gabe trudged into the kitchen, shoelaces trailing from his boat-size high-tops. "School bus's here." He grabbed his lunch sack and disappeared. Rafe followed.

"Rafe, your lunch!" Mitch lobbed the brown bag to him through the doorway. Shortly after, he heard them thunder down the front stairs.

"Mitch, you'll have to walk Michael to school when he's ready. Seri, let's go." Ellie scooped up her book bag and followed her daughter.

"Please don't forget to fix my dollhouse," Seri yelled as she trotted down the back stairs.

Mitch opened the oven door and handed Ellie the egg sandwich he'd been keeping warm. Two weeks had made it clear to him she *never* left time to take care of herself.

"Oh." Her eyes widened with surprise.

"Don't make a mess in the car," he grumbled.

Her cheeks colored, but one honey-colored brow

notched upward. She looked completely unflappable, right down to that rare curve of her soft pink lips.

She looked amused.

Mitch almost growled.

"I'll be home as soon as my final's over. In time to fix lunch." For the first time in a week, she looked him straight in the eyes. Then she was gone.

The room felt empty.

"I'm hungry."

Mitch turned in time to catch Michael lifting the little black terrier onto a stool. The kid climbed onto the next stool and dug into the eggs Rafe had rejected. Stretching forward precariously, the dog snatched a bite, too.

"Hey! Dog on the floor. Here, I'll fix you some fresh eggs." Mitch tried to grab the plate, but Michael hung on.

"It's okay. Bubba's our baby-sitter. Besides, I like cold eggs. I like cold pizza and cold tacos, but I like chocolate milk hot." He fed another chunk of egg to Bubba Sue. "And I like fried ice cream."

Mitch came around the counter and set the dog on the floor. "Baby-sitters with wet noses eat on the floor. She can have those eggs. I'll make you more."

"I can eat these." Michael hastily filled his mouth. "I had my cootie shot," he mumbled around the food.

"Cootie shot?"

Michael wiped his mouth on his sleeve. "Hold out your arm."

Giving up on the eggs, Mitch stretched out his arm.

With his index finger, Michael drew on Mitch's forearm. "Circle, circle. Dot, dot. Now you've had your cootie shot. Means you can't catch anything from Bubba Sue. It keeps girls away, too."

Mitch rubbed his arm. "Thanks. Just what I needed."

If the kid had an inoculation against a short, tantalizing little mother of four, Mitch would be in great shape.

As it was, each day he was losing more ground.

The doorbell rang.

"Mrs. Givens!" Michael spun from the stool.

Mitch raced him to the door, losing to both boy and dog by a nose.

"Mrs. Givens, am I glad—"

"What are *you* doing home, young man?" The hefty white-haired woman stepped in and put a wrist to Michael's forehead. "Hmm, no fever. This boy should be in school, Mr. Kole. Go get ready." Smiling, she gave Michael a pat on the behind.

"Okay." He skipped across the room with the dog following. Halfway down the hall, boy and pet stopped. "I need two dollars for a field trip."

"You got it." Mitch turned back to Mrs. Givens with a sheepish shrug.

"Mr. Kole, your father's not doing as well as I'd like."

"I know. Will he have to go back to the hospital?"

"Hey!" Michael bounded into the room tugging a T-shirt over his head. "I forgot, I need three dozen cookies."

"*When?*"

"Today."

Mitch groaned.

"They sell wonderful cookies at the KirkKnoll Bakery, Mr. Kole. And, to answer your question, your father needs more attention. From now on, I want you and Ellie to work with him at least three times a day."

Three times? Where was Ellie going to find more time?

The phone rang.

"I can see you're busy, Mr. Kole. I'll talk with you after I've finished King's morning therapy."

Muttering, Mitch strode to the kitchen. "Michael, *what* are you *doing?*"

Michael laid the phone on the counter. "Some lady wants to come by the store early."

"You told her the store opens at ten, right?"

"Yep, but I told her she could come earlier and ring the doorbell."

"*Mi*-chael…!" Mitch shoved a hand through his hair. He did pretty well with kids on the ski slopes, but taking care of Ellie's four kids wasn't the same as teaching *twenty* kids to ski. Skiing lessons only lasted an hour!

"Just go get ready for school, okay?"

"Okay. I think I'll wear my Tazz jacket, but maybe I'll wear my…" He disappeared down the hall.

Mitch seriously reconsidered punching the cupboard. Instead he gathered up the dirty dishes, relishing every clink and clatter as he piled them into the sink.

He'd gotten himself into a real mess here. This particular kitchen was getting way too hot. Swiping a sleeve across his brow, he leaned against the counter. Behind him something swished to the floor. Squatting, he gathered up three tissue flowers, a brochure and some scraps of paper.

The crazy tissue flowers were all over the darn house. He tossed them into the basket on the counter. What about the brochure?

Community College Summer Session Course Schedule. So. He laid the torn scraps of paper on the counter, fitting the ragged edges together. Ellie had been planning to go to summer school, he realized, but she'd torn up her class choices. She was giving up school to stay home with King, postponing the education that would give her and her kids their independence. His guilt meter swung into the red zone.

For a long moment, he stared out the window. Ellie shouldn't have to handle so many things by herself. She shouldn't have to put her life on hold for King. Hunting through the drawers, he found a roll of tape and stuck the pieces back together. Then he folded the paper and stuffed it into his shirt pocket.

Turning, he studied the calendar on the refrigerator. Two more weeks. Ellie had King's doctor appointment marked in red! He took a deep breath. Said several words he knew Ellie wouldn't approve. There were things here that needed to be set right before his month's sentence ended. As soon as Ellie returned, he'd get started.

Ellie hurried down the back stairs, trying to put distance between her and Mitch. Ducking into the store, she scanned quickly, spotting Robin ringing a sale at the cash register. Thank goodness some college students were willing to work part-time for not much money.

Thank goodness Ellie wouldn't be in the store with Mitch alone.

She glanced back at him. "The tools are in the storage closet. I hope you can fix that bathroom faucet."

"Ellie, we need to talk."

Just keep moving, she told herself. The last time Mitch had used that tone with her, she'd ended up kissing him. Shamelessly. Wonderfully. Not something she could ever let happen again.

"Don't have time to talk now." Or any time the rest of this century! Somehow she'd managed to avoid being alone with him since The Night of the Kiss, though she hadn't really wanted to. It wasn't a whole lot easier being around him with other people—especially her children. He was so gentle with Seri and Rafe. So patient with Michael. So accepting in the face of Gabe's back talk.

She was getting too close, too close to wanting Mitch around all the time. If she could just last another two weeks...

"That was a good sale, Ms. Sander." Robin closed the register drawer.

"Thanks, Rob. You can leave now."

"Okay. By the way, some rental instruments were returned this morning. I didn't have time to get them all shelved. And those boxes arrived."

Ellie glanced back to where Robin pointed. She was surprised to see Mitch had already hoisted the largest box to his shoulder.

"Long as you've got me for slave labor, where do you want these, Ellie?"

"Just put them in the storage room."

Mitch grinned, then ducked through the door.

Bells on the front door jingled as Ellie waved Robin out. The sound lingered as she counted the boxes still to be moved. Four more and Mitch would go back upstairs to fix the faucet. Four more and she could relax.

Mitch reappeared in the doorway. "Storage room's pretty disorganized, Ellie. Want to show me where you want these?"

No, she did not. Sighing, she retraced her steps to the back and peered into the small room. Several instruments in cases lay on the floor. Mitch had begun returning them to the shelves.

"Hope the system hasn't changed since I worked here. Did I put these on the right shelves?"

Reluctantly she stepped inside to check. "You seem to be doing fine."

Brushing by her, he hefted a tuba case to the top shelf by the door. "When Yuba played the tuba down in Cuba..." he sang as he passed, grinning down at her.

She was in dangerous territory here in this small room with Mitch. Too much aware of him and whatever it was that hummed between them. "Just put the boxes over there when you finish." She turned to leave, but Mitch stepped between her and the door.

Before she realized what was happening, he reached down and nuzzled her neck.

Shivers exploded all over her. "Mitch, if you don't move, I'll—"

"Okay, okay, just couldn't resist." Grinning, he stepped back. "Ellie, we need to talk. About this."

Suddenly he was all seriousness. He pulled a piece of paper from his shirt pocket and handed it to her.

The paper had been crudely taped together, but she recognized it—her class schedule for next semester. She thought she'd thrown it away.

"There's nothing to talk about. King needs someone home with him full-time till he heals." She moved toward the doorway.

Mitch stopped her. "You don't need to give up your classes. I can hire someone."

She never should have let him trap her in here. Raising her chin, she fixed him with a stern gaze.

He didn't budge. "I'm not moving till you promise you'll go to school next semester."

She had to get away—from his outdoor scent, from the warmth that radiated from him. From her own wanting.

"King needs someone who cares about him." She

saw his flicker of guilt. It was the break she needed. "Would you please let me by."

He hesitated. For a moment she thought he'd refuse.

Slowly he stepped aside. "You're a very determined woman, Ellie Sander."

"Don't ever forget it." She slipped by him to the safety of the store. Peter had called her stubborn. When it came to people she loved, she could be downright mule-headed.

She tried to focus on adding the morning's receipts from the cash register, but her hands still shook. She was too aware of Mitch carrying the boxes into the storage room, shuffling around inside. If he would just go back up to the flat. Away from her.

"All finished, Ellie," he called. "But I don't see the tools."

"On the shelf...by the door."

"Not there."

She puffed out a breath and marched across the store. She would show him the tools, but she wouldn't let him trap her again. Stopping just outside the doorway, she leaned in and pointed. "They're right—" The space on the shelf was empty.

Hazarding a step inside, she searched along the shelf. "I'm sure I put them right—"

Behind her, Mitch closed the door.

"What are you *doing?* Mitch, don't start this again. What if someone comes into the *store?*"

"The bells will jingle." Taking her chin in his hand, he tilted her face up to him.

The gesture caught her off guard. Made her go light-headed and weak. Made her forget to resist. Her gaze flew to his mouth. But it was set in a stern line.

"Ellie, for just a minute, I want you to listen to me.

You're trying to do too much. You study all night, take finals all morning, cook, look after King…'' He ended his tirade, his gaze traveling to her lips.

Ellie held her breath. This shouldn't be happening. ''Mitch, please…''

He straightened a little. ''You handle the store, run interference with your kids…and manage to look…too damn tempting for any man to resist.''

She tried to protest, but he raised a finger to her lips, sending a tremor through her.

''But you've also got circles under your eyes, and you're too thin, and—'' he searched her face ''—King's not the only one around here who needs some looking after.''

The concern in his eyes sent regret shimmering through her. Mitch was right. What she needed was a man who would help her, who would share with her and care with her, hug her when she was hurting and make love to her even when they were both frazzled and exhausted from their responsibilities.

But Mitch wasn't that kind of man.

''Ellie, I think you should get in touch with your—''

She put her hand to his chest—to keep herself from kissing him anyhow. ''Mitch, I *am* in touch. I know exactly what I'm doing.''

''No, Ellie, I mean—''

She stepped back, using her anger to hide how much she wanted him. ''I think this is very presumptuous of you, Mitch—*you* telling *me* what to do with my life. Especially since you can hardly wait to get back to Colorado!''

Silence. He looked as if she'd slapped him. Slowly he stepped aside. Opened the storage room door.

Ellie hadn't known she could still feel such pain. Someone else's pain.

Reaching up, he pulled the tools from an upper shelf. "You're right, Ellie. Time to go do something I know how to do."

Chapter Five

Mitch trudged up the back stairs, feeling about a thousand years old. The tools he lugged had to weigh at least a hundred pounds.

At the top of the stairs, he plodded into the kitchen, crossed to the coffeemaker, poured a cup of cold, murky liquid and set it in the microwave.

He could warm a second cup and take it back down to Ellie. He'd much rather be in the store with her than up here fixing a leaky faucet.

But she'd all but thrown him out of the store. From her *life*, he reminded himself. And banishment was what he deserved. Banishment was what he needed. He shouldn't have held her captive in the instrument closet. He should have found a better way to appeal to her about her parents.

When it came to Ellie, he didn't seem to use very good judgment.

Through the kitchen door, the volume of the TV rose by decibels. Mitch glanced into the front room, then pulled back. Michael and Rafe were home from school already. If Michael discovered Mitch, the kid would start talking again. He'd want to help fix the faucet, and he'd ask about a million questions. The thought made Mitch's head pound.

He did a quick mental inventory. Gabe hadn't appeared from baseball practice yet, and the last time he'd peeked in on Seri she'd seemed as happy as a real princess, spread out on the floor in King's bedroom with her repaired dollhouse. If she knew Mitch had come upstairs, she'd want to play, and he didn't think he could handle another game of make-believe right now. He'd already engaged in too much fantasy about Ellie.

The black mood he'd been nursing all day settled back in.

At least he didn't have to think about King for an hour or two. They'd already done his afternoon "workout." King would probably rest until dinner.

Unfortunately resting was all King seemed to want to do these days. He'd only talked to Mitch once this afternoon—when he'd caught him making a list of everything that still needed fixing.

Your mother used to make lists, King had muttered.

Another thing Mitch had forgotten—King used to tease his mother about her lists. He'd teased her a lot when he'd been home. Made her laugh. Made her happy. So many things Mitch seemed to have forgotten from those days.

He glared at the humming microwave, at the basket of paper flowers on the counter. He checked the bag of plumbing supplies he'd bought on his return from walking Michael to school. Beneath his feet, the floor vibrated, and he pictured Ellie moving around in the store downstairs.

Things were getting real bad when the rattle of a closing door made him think of her. It was about time he
put his mind to something more productive. Doggedly
he gathered his plumbing supplies and coffee and plodded down the hall with his dark cloud.

He was almost past the Mermaid Room when he
slowed to a stop. Strange…he thought he heard music.
As if someone were improvising on a keyboard. The
bedroom door stood ajar. He hesitated, then pushed it
open.

In the far corner, Gabe sat hunched over an electronic
keyboard, his fingers coaxing a melody from the keys—
from the sound of it, an old Beatles song.

Gabe was playing Mitch's old Vox! King must have
kept it after Mitch left. The realization filled him with
surprising pleasure.

The kid played pretty well. How old was he? Ten?
His old man might not have been much of a father, but
he'd taught Gabe to play. The kid had talent. Looked as
though he loved it, too.

Mitch huffed silently at the irony of the scene. He'd
been here, done this—poured his adolescent angst into
music in this very room, just as Gabe was doing.

Abruptly the music stopped. Gabe stood, knocking the
bench over backward.

"Hey, you don't have to quit. You sounded good."
But Mitch spoke too late. Glaring at him, Gabe rushed
across the room, pushing by to disappear through the
door.

Mitch's dark cloud blackened. No point in going after
him. Gabe didn't want anything to do with him; he'd
made that clear from the beginning. Still, he hated to see
the kid struggle. Adolescence was such a painful time—

he could still remember. But Gabe would never believe Mitch understood.

He dropped the plumbing supplies on the bed and bent to right the bench. On impulse, he slid onto it, and let his gaze roam the familiar instrument. At last, he set his coffee aside and settled his fingers onto the keys. The notes came hesitantly at first.

Slowly the songs came back to him. How many hours had he played this thing, full of confusion and anger…and grief? Memories weren't supposed to be this painful.

A movement in the doorway caught his eye. Gabe slouched against the door frame.

So the kid hadn't fled after all. The lure of the music was stronger than his need to rebel. That hadn't been true for Mitch.

He continued to play. "Back when I first got this thing, it was considered the best."

"*You?* That's King's."

"King plays a lot of instruments, but this one was mine. Got my initials on it."

"No way."

"Suit yourself." Mitch began improvising rhythms.

Gabe inched back into the room, shuffling nearer until he peered over Mitch's shoulder at the silvery monogram.

Mitch ran a finger over the letters. "*MJK*. Mitchell James Kole. That's me."

"If it's yours, why's it *here?*" Gabe demanded.

Mitch couldn't very well tell Gabe he'd left the gift from his father behind when he'd run away. He *had* been almost seventeen, but numbers wouldn't mean much to a hurt ten-year-old. Mitch didn't need to give the kid ideas.

"I...didn't have time for it with my job." He continued to improvise, sensing that Gabe itched to play again.

Michael burst into the room. "Hey! Who's playing?"

Mitch missed a beat.

"I thought it was *you,* Gabe." Michael trotted over. "I thought you were gonna get in trouble. Look, Rafe, it's Mitch!"

Mitch glanced up to find Rafe standing in the doorway holding the ever-present portable phone. Accompanied by the ever-present tail-thumping Bubba Sue.

Somehow he wasn't surprised when Seri showed up, too. She squirmed around Rafe and darted over, resting her hand on Mitch's arm as she smiled up at him. His dark cloud seemed to fade.

Changing keys, he began a song he thought they might know. Sure enough, Seri started to hum.

Gabe sneered. "That's a *girl's* song."

Seri clapped her hands and began to sing. Michael joined in. Even Rafe drifted nearer.

How to engage Gabe? Mitch cued into another song he was pretty sure Gabe would reject.

"Du-uh." Gabe jeered.

Right on target. Mitch squelched a grin. "So name something else."

"'Yellow Submarine.'"

Mitch fiddled around playing wrong notes.

"You don't even know it. Move, I'll show you."

Mitch started to get up, but Gabe slid in beside him, concentrating on the keys. Quickly he found the melody, and Michael and Seri sang along.

"Hey, you guys are good." Taking a chance, Mitch tried a couple of bass chords, adjusted the tuning knobs and waited for Gabe to storm away.

Instead Gabe watched him closely. "Cool."

That was all Mitch needed. Leaning forward, he added bass to Gabe's melody. Rafe laid the phone on the worn old desk, pulled a couple of pencils from a cup and began tapping out the rhythm.

Someone was singing harmony. Mitch turned. Michael never did anything harmoniously...but he was doing it now!

"You kids have talent."

Seri beamed. "We can do 'Hey Jude.' Gabe, play 'Hey Jude'!"

"Don't play another note!"

Suddenly the room fell into stunned silence. Mitch turned in unison with the four kids. The arrival of one angry mom had turned them into guilty conspirators.

Ellie marched into the room like a drill sergeant. She looked furious—and scared.

Storm clouds were regathering fast. If Mitch didn't act, they were due for a bad patch of weather.

"Ellie! Come on in. The kids found my old key—"

"Don't say another word." Clapping a hand at her waist, she pointed to the door with the other.

"I want you four Sanders out of here, *immediately*." She fixed them each with a stern glare as they slouched past.

"Ellie, they weren't causing any harm."

She whirled to glare at him. "I'll be the judge of harm, Mitchell Kole."

"But, Mo-om—"

"No 'but Moms,' Gabe." Her tone softened ever so slightly as she watched Gabe shuffle after the other three.

Maybe she was relenting. Maybe he could talk her out of punishing the kids.

"Ellie, I was the one who encouraged—"

She swung around to confront him. "I don't want to

hear it, Mitch. From now on, *just leave my children alone.*"

Ellie turned away, wishing she could send Mitch out of her life—out of her kids' lives—right now. She should have known. He was just another spell-weaving musician. *Magician* would be more accurate. Creator of illusions.

"Ellie, wait. Give me a chance to explain."

She stopped herself from clapping her hands over her ears to block out Mitch's persuasive appeal. Magicians were good at that, smooth-talking while they worked their magic.

"There's nothing to explain." She spun toward the door after her retreating children, but he grasped her wrist and swung her back.

She landed in his arms. Flattening her palms against his shirtfront, she fought the impulse to fold herself into his embrace.

Mitch made her want to be held and protected. His touch made her want to be sheltered and kissed.

But she couldn't let that happen again. With every ounce of her will, she pushed away and backed toward the door.

"I *should* have known... You *are* King's son, after all. Anyone else would have guessed right away you were musical. I never should have told you about The Angels—"

"Ellie, Gabe found the keyboard. I stumbled in on his playing." Mitch moved toward her, hand outstretched, his eyes full of entreaty. "I could see how he loves it."

She backed away, matching his steps one for one. "He doesn't love it. He loves a dream. He has to give it up."

"Why does he have to give it up? It's the first time I've seen him happy since I got here."

No. She didn't want that to be true. "His father made promises, Mitch. He told them Peter Angelo and The Angels would be famous. He told them they'd make CD's and do TV and win Grammy's... He was going to *use* them...to make up for his own...shortcomings. He worked them and worked them...and when they weren't good enough, he ran out." She took another step back, reaching for the doorway. "I won't let them be hurt like that again. *Ever!*"

Suddenly she could retreat no farther; she'd backed into the wall.

Mitch closed the distance between them, resting his hands against the wall on either side of her.

"Ellie, I would never hurt your kids."

She couldn't stop herself from looking up at him, from getting lost in his eyes. He was so big, so darkly handsome. So overpowering. His eyes clouded, with concern...or passion, she couldn't tell. She couldn't even think. She only knew her heart raced, and she wanted him to kiss her. And she couldn't let him.

"You told them they had talent."

He leaned nearer, his brows knotting in an anguished frown. "*You* heard them, Ellie. They *do*."

His heat swirled around her. His scent made her weak. She closed her eyes, blotting out his image. Sliding her hands behind her back, she stopped herself from reaching out to him.

"And you're just another man who'll make them dream...." She paused to will the tremor from her voice. It was better for them not to keep fairy-tale dreams, not to believe in happy endings.

Gathering all her courage, she opened her eyes. "...and then you'll *leave.*"

She could see his struggle. It was all she could do to keep from rising on her tiptoes and reaching up to kiss him. She knew he would kiss her back, kiss her thoroughly, kiss her until she forgot everything.

But eventually, they would regain their senses. And then?

Mitch's arms dropped slowly to his sides.

She was right, and he knew it. She could see it in his eyes. In two weeks, he would be gone.

"I won't let anyone hurt my children again," she whispered. *I won't let anyone hurt me, either.*

Ellie carried the cookies to the dinner table, too much aware that Mitch wouldn't look at her. Holding the plate with both hands, she fought off her shakiness. They had watched her through the entire meal, her children, King—everyone but Mitch. None of them had broken the silence. Even the soft-hearted little dog lay under the table with the unwaggingest tail she'd ever seen.

Ellie knew just how Bubba Sue felt. How was she ever going to get through the two weeks Mitch had left?

She hurried to the far end of the table. "Cookie, King? Mitch brought them from the bakery."

King shook his head, waved the plate away.

Ellie's heart sank. If this meal were an example, she didn't know how *any* of them would make it.

They didn't make a pretty picture. Gabe had shot verbal barbs at Mitch all through dinner, and Rafe had called Information to ask for his father's telephone number. Poor little Seri looked so lost, searching everyone's face for some kind of reassurance. And Michael...! Her loquacious son hadn't said one word since she'd run him out of the bedroom that afternoon.

Worst of all, neither her children nor King had even acknowledged the tissue flowers she'd laid at their places before dinner.

King's silence worried her most of all.

As for Mitch, he wouldn't look at her because he *knew* she was right. He needed to stay out of their lives. Setting the cookies in front of him, she beat a fast retreat.

"If Mitch gets a cookie, does that mean he isn't in trouble anymore?" Seri's small voice rang with hopefulness.

Ellie imagined a collective sigh rising around the table, as if Seri's words had broken a spell.

"It just means he ate all his dinner."

"I ate all mine, too. I had a leg and a thigh and I ate some broccoli, just like King, and—"

"Michael..." Ellie breathed her own sigh of relief. Her son was talking again—even if it was the excessive prattle he'd started since his father left.

"So can I have double cookies, Mom, please, can I?"

"You can have the same as everyone else, Michael."

"Rules don't seem to have changed much since I was your age, guys," Mitch drawled. "But maybe I better skip cookies tonight. I never *used* to get them when I was in the doghouse."

Ellie caught her breath. She shouldn't have looked at him. She'd been crazy to think Mitch would stay repentant about this afternoon. She should have known that smile would steal back into his eyes and dance around the corners of his mouth. The man was incapable of remorse. He was incorrigible.

"Mitch isn't in trouble. He's just..."

King cleared his throat. "Harriet asked about KirkKnoll Days today."

Heads swung in his direction. Ellie slumped back in her chair, but relief flew away when she looked up. Mitch was watching her again. One dark brow cocked upward as if to say, "What *am* I, Ellie."

Irresistible came immediately to mind. Omigod. She puffed a breath into her bangs as heat swept up her neck. "KirkKnoll Days?" she blurted.

"Uh-hmm," King mumbled. "She wanted to know who's teaching the Kole Kids this year."

Mitch's gaze wavered. "The Kole Kids?"

"King Kole's Kids," Michael said between bites of cookie. "They sing for this neighborhood show. It's called KirkKnoll Days, Mom. It's at the park. Our teacher told us."

For once Ellie didn't stop Michael's chatter. Anything to divert Mitch's attention.

"It's for Remembering Day weekend, and there'll be a parade and clowns and rides and—"

"*Memorial* Day, Mike." King chuckled. "Mitch and his mother used to go to the festivities every year. When I was home, we went together."

King had laughed! Ellie sat up straighter. "Will they be singing this year?" Maybe if she and Mitch could get King out to see them...

"No." King stared down at his casts. "I had to let the kids down. Plastic leg irons don't travel well to rehearsals."

Seri squirmed in her chair. "Mom...?"

"Surely there's someone who can teach them."

Seri tugged Ellie's sleeve. *"Mom?"*

"The other musicians in the area have their own performers."

Here's a HOT offer for you!

Get set for a sizzling summer read...

with **2 FREE ROMANCE BOOKS**

and a **FREE MYSTERY GIFT!**

NO CATCH! NO OBLIGATION TO BUY!

Simply complete and return this card and you'll get **FREE BOOKS, A FREE GIFT** and much more!

- The first shipment is yours to keep, absolutely free!
- Enjoy the convenience of romance books, delivered right to your door, before they're available in the stores!
- Take advantage of special low pricing for Reader Service Members only!
- After receiving your free books we hope you'll want to remain a subscriber. But the choice is always yours—to continue or cancel anytime at all! So why not take us up on this fabulous invitation with no risk of any kind. You'll be glad you did!

315 SDL CPSQ

**215 SDL CPSH
S-R-05/99**

▼ DETACH HERE AND MAIL CARD TODAY! ▼

Name:		
	(Please Print)	
Address:		Apt.#:
City:		
State/Prov.:		Zip/Postal Code:

The Silhouette Reader Service™ —Here's How it Works:

Accepting your 2 free books and mystery gift places you under no obligation to buy anything. You may keep the books and gift and return the shipping statement marked "cancel." If you do not cancel, about a month later we'll send you 6 additional novels and bill you just $2.90 each in the U.S., or $3.25 each in Canada, plus 25¢ delivery per book and applicable taxes if any.* That's the complete price and — compared to the cover price of $3.50 in the U.S. and $3.99 in Canada — it's quite a bargain! You may cancel at any time, but if you choose to continue, every month we'll send you 6 more books, which you may either purchase at the discount price or return to us and cancel your subscription.

*Terms and prices subject to change without notice. Sales tax applicable in N.Y. Canadian residents will be charged applicable provincial taxes and GST.

If offer card is missing write to: Silhouette Reader Service, 3010 Walden Ave., P.O. Box 1867, Buffalo, NY 14240-1867

"*Mo*-om," Seri hollered. "Mitch could teach them!"

Mitch shoved back from the table. "I...don't think so." His napkin fell to the floor.

Ellie watched him in surprise. Mitch had gone all edgy. He'd clearly gotten her message this afternoon. But that didn't mean he couldn't make music with other kids.

"*Yes!*" Michael gestured in the air with his fist. "Mitch plays good, and he knows lots of songs."

Hope nudged Ellie's heart. If Mitch took on this job for King—

"He could do it," Seri exclaimed. "He could teach them for you, *couldn't* he, King?"

"I believe he could," King murmured.

Ellie's spirits rose. There was light in King's eyes for the first time in ages. He was almost smiling.

Mitch gave a strangled cough. Edged away from the table.

"Here." She thrust the plate of cookies at him before he could bolt. "Sit down and eat your dessert."

If Mitch taught the Kole Kids, it would keep him busy his last two weeks here. Keep him out of her life. Out of the storage closet. Away from her kids.

Maybe the strange tension between Mitch and his father could be resolved. Most important, maybe it would help King get well.

Ellie fixed Mitch with a firm gaze. "I think Seri has a great idea. It's a sure way to get you out of the doghouse."

Mitch flinched, but he couldn't ignore Ellie's excitement. How had she done this? One minute, he thought he'd get through the next two weeks just working with King and fixing things up around the place. Staying away from Ellie and her kids. The next minute, he was being offered the Mutt of the Year award by a crafty Cheshire cat. Except that Ellie looked more like a kitten—a soft, purring kitten. Which was exactly why he was in serious trouble. Had been since the first time he'd laid eyes on her.

"Look, there's already more to do around here than we can all keep up with."

Ellie's blue eyes widened with innocence. "I've been getting all *my* work done," she crooned. "You guys having trouble keeping up?"

"Huh-uh," Seri exclaimed.

"Nope," Michael declared.

"Not me." Even Rafe spoke up.

"But with Mrs. Givens upping King's workouts to three a day—"

"I'm done with school. I'll have lots of extra time." She beamed at him prettily, but he read "Gotcha," in her eyes.

"The Prince can do anything." Seri stood beside his chair, peering up at him with those big, expressive eyes. Like her mother's, yet so dark and grave.

"You know, son, I was going to use some of those Beatles songs you liked so well…"

Mitch felt the old defenses kick in. This was the first time King had shown interest in anything since he'd come home. But Mitch hadn't come back to take care of his father's…commitments.

"I haven't played in years. I doubt I'd remember any of them."

King's brows rose. "The nut doesn't fall that far from the tree, son. Bet you could finish any song I started."

Because most of them were songs King had taught him. Music he'd loved until… He glanced again at Ellie.

Her full mouth curved into that almost-smile. Her eyes held a fragile hope.

Hey, he couldn't take on the responsibility of teaching a bunch of kids. He was King's son. As the twig is bent...King broke commitments. At least Mitch had learned not to make them.

Except that this was a broken promise King was *suffering* from. Something else Mitch didn't remember about his father.

"Did *you* play at KirkKnoll Days, Mitch?" Gabe demanded, tilting his chair to its back legs.

Damn. Why did the kid have to stir up memories like that?

King sat forward in his chair. "You bet he did, Gabe. He played keyboard one year with my band. He was a big hit."

Mitch looked away from the pleasure in King's eyes. The keyboard had been new that year. The dreamed-of Vox Super Continental, a birthday present—played on the biggest day of his thirteen-year-old life. How could he have forgotten?

Pushing the memories aside, he met Gabe's glare. "Will *you kids* perform at KirkKnoll Days?"

Gabe slammed the chair back down. Grabbing the tissue flower lying by his plate, he twirled it around and around. "Nah." His voice lacked its usual bite.

Seri reached up and tugged Mitch's sleeve.

"Wait... Seri... What are you—?" Before he could stop her, she'd squirmed into his lap.

"Mom only lets us sing at school and church." Her wistful tone matched the appeal in her eyes.

What was he supposed to do *now?* In all his thirty-five years, he'd never held a little kid in his lap. It made him feel kind of…mushy inside. What was he supposed to do with his hands?

He settled for clutching the arms of the chair, then stole another glance at Ellie. She was frowning. Probably cooking up another rule—no fairy tales, no music and now no Princess in his lap. He checked around the table. Everyone was staring at him—except Gabe.

But Gabe's head rose until he looked squarely at Mitch. "You can't lead singers and play at the same time."

"I'm not going to lead—" Mitch stammered to a halt. This wasn't one of Gabe's usual snipes. He was reaching out. Asking for something.

"Please, Prince?" Seri whispered. Gently she settled her sticky palms right on his cheeks. She looked like a forlorn little waif.

The kids wanted to perform. Gabe wanted to play. Not on TV, not for a Grammy, but just for the fun of a neighborhood show. Mitch might not know squat about kids, but this sounded pretty positive to him. Pretty healthy.

Damn, he was two notes short of an octave to even consider it. What did he know about teaching kids to sing? He didn't even *like* kids.

What did he know about the Sander kids? That they had the most loving, self-sacrificing, valiant little mother in the world. That Ellie loved them wholly and unselfishly. That they'd lost their other parent.

He understood all that far too well.

Drawing in a deep breath, he tucked a wisp of dove brown hair behind Seri's ear. Smiled weakly at Ellie. Maybe doing this for King would help him heal. Maybe it was time they all started to heal.

"Okay. I'll do it."

A chorus of shouts blasted him. Cringing, he held up his hands. "On one condition."

The room fell silent. Ellie's head tilted. Her blue eyes narrowed with suspicion, with that distrust her former husband had left behind.

"What condition?" she demanded.

"That the Sander kids sing, too. That they join the Kole Kids. Maybe Gabe could play."

Seri's squeal nearly deafened him as she threw her arms around his neck. Michael bounced across the floor, Bubba Sue barking at his heels. Rafe tapped a rhythm on the table. And Gabe? Hey, the kid *could* smile, after all.

But Ellie looked as if he'd just slapped her. He was back to being the enemy.

Enemy was good, he reminded himself. Enemies didn't get kisses. Right now she looked as if she'd rather kill him. He needed to insure things stayed that way.

"One more condition." He might as well make hay while the sun shone, because things were going to get pretty stormy pretty quick.

"What's that, son?" King was actually smiling.

"That Ellie sign up for those summer classes."

She clamped her mouth shut and glared at him. He could almost read her thoughts. Summer school wasn't the issue here. Her children were.

She turned away to gaze at her children; he'd seen her do it before when she looked exhausted and uncertain. As if she could draw strength from their innocence and trust. She had no one else, he reminded himself. Not even parents who were available with love and support.

But right now, her kids' eyes held excitement. Pleading.

"Will you, Mom? Will you go to summer school? If you're going to be a dentist, you really *should* go."

Michael—that little smarty—had drawn Ellie's attention away from the real issue and then *stopped talking*. The first real self-control Mitch had seen in the kid.

"We wouldn't get paid or anything, Mom. It'd be just for fun."

Gabe—sounding realistic—almost like an adult instead of some alien teenage creature.

"We wouldn't have to watch TV after school."

Rafe. So young to be a pragmatist. For the first time since Mitch had arrived, the boy had forgotten the portable phone.

"Mitch makes mistakes, Mom."

Seri. A four-year-old assuring her mom The Prince would never make it to the big time. Mitch stifled a smile. He hadn't given the kid enough credit.

"It's not a professional show, Ellie."

His own father adding a vote. Mitch waited for his anger to rise. This was the one wound too great for healing. But for once King's words didn't feel like betrayal.

So. The vote was unanimous. Except for Ellie.

He never should have looked at her again, because anguish creased her brow, and her eyes darkened with conflict. She reached for the paper flower beside Rafe's plate.

Crazy paper flowers, showing up at the darnedest times. Ellie looked so vulnerable plucking at its torn edges. She looked so young. So alone. It hurt him to see her that way.

Damn. He'd done this to her, made her choose between people she loved. Would she let her cherished children perform, in spite of all her fears for them? Would she say no and watch King continue to languish?

Mitch was some Prince of a guy, all right.

Ellie looked up at him. Her chin rose that wondrous little fraction. "Any other conditions, Maestro?"

Guilt threatened to swamp him. She was stalling, this hardheaded little woman. She was so damned proud. And he was about to go for broke.

He offered a sheepish half grin—and the final straw. "That you invite your parents to come see their grandkids perform."

The flower in her hand stilled. So did everyone in the room. The blue of her eyes sparked with anger, but he couldn't stop looking at her. She was so pretty. So incredibly strong.

He knew the second she decided, because she hitched her chin up that queenly little notch—and delivered his sentence.

"Okay, Mitch. You got yourself a job. I suggest you start tomorrow because you haven't got much time."

Shouts burst around the table, and Seri planted a wet kiss on his cheek. Mitch braced for the warning that had kept him out of trouble all these years: *Don't make commitments you won't keep.* But his alarm system seemed to have shut down.

Terror gripped him. Mitchell James Kole, black diamond skier and Rocky Mountain rescuer, survivor of blizzards, avalanches and bored rich heiresses, suddenly *wanted* to help his father get well. Wanted Ellie's kids to heal. Was taking on a commitment he had to keep. All because of Ellie.

That was the most terrifying of all.

Chapter Six

"They're here!" Seri squealed.

Ellie's pulse leapt. She swiped her damp hands on the backside of her crisply ironed jeans and checked her family one last time. She wanted her four wonderful children to be absolutely perfect for their grandparents.

Seri looked precious in her new rose pink dress, standing so still at the flat's front windows. Much as Ellie hated to admit it, her daughter did resemble a princess. Because of her curls, of course. For her first visit with Grandma and Grandpa, Seri wasn't about to bounce those reluctant ringlets out.

And dear Rafe, such a little man in the white, button-down shirt he'd picked out at the discount store. But he was still kid enough to press his nose against the glass. Still missing his daddy enough to guard the portable phone, Ellie thought ruefully.

Then there was Michael. Where he got his energy, she'd never know. Just watching him and the dog hop up and down the top two steps of the stairway wore her out.

"Michael, remember what I said."

"I know, Mom. I'm just practicing."

If she managed to keep him from dashing down the stairs to show off his new hockey Blues T-shirt, it would be a miracle.

She saw Gabe scoot to the edge of the sofa, then think better of getting up. He slouched back into place, tugged at a loose thread on the hem of his new St. Louis Cardinals T-shirt. She could tell he was scared.

So was she.

Now that Mitch had forced the issue, she really wanted to put her differences with her father behind. She wanted so much to see her parents again, wanted her kids to know their grandparents. But she and her brood weren't exactly a country club kind of crew. What if her father took one look at them and decided he didn't want anything to do with them? What if her mother changed her mind, too?

The doorbell chimed.

Ellie's pulse clutched again as Bubba Sue began to bark.

"Okay, everybody—on the sofa with Gabe. Best behavior, now. Grandma and Grandpa are going to love you."

Oh, please, let it be true. She wiped her palms on her jeans once more as she descended the stairs. At the bottom, she closed her eyes. *Please let everything be okay.* She dragged in a deep breath and opened the door.

"Mom? Dad?"

"Ellie, sweetheart!"

Then she was in her mother's arms, and they were hugging and crying and laughing.

"Hello, Ellen."

There was no mistaking her father's starched voice, even at such an emotional reunion. The air suddenly felt crisp.

"Dad!" She turned to him as eagerly as she had her mother, but hugging her father was like hugging a telephone pole. Ellie stepped back, fighting a different kind of tears, struggling for a smile. "It's good to see you," she murmured. She had to keep believing things were going to be good.

"Let me look at you." Her mother stepped back to survey her. "Oh, Ellie, you're so thin!"

"And you look wonderful, Mom!" She did—still slender and athletic in her navy skirt and matched sweater set, her short, wavy hair shining a champagne shade of blond. The color King called granny gold! "I like the color of your hair.

"And, Dad, you're in great shape, as always." Still trim and square-shouldered in his navy sports coat, still square-jawed and stern. But his salt-and-pepper hair had turned white at the temples, giving him an even greater aura of authority. He looked positively formidable.

Ellie squared her own shoulders. In the past eleven years, she'd learned a thing or two about toughness herself.

"I'm so glad you're here." She linked arms with her father. "I missed you so much. And the kids can hardly wait to see you. I'm surprised they haven't bolted down here already."

"Oh, Ellie, we missed you, too." Her mother wiped tears from her cheeks, then took Ellie's hand. "Let's go see them right now. Gordon, please bring the bag. I brought presents for everyone. I just hope they like…"

"*Four* children," her father said, following them up

the stairs. "Too damn young...never should have eloped..."

Disheartened, Ellie hurried ahead, hoping her father's attitude would change when they were all together. She'd threatened her children with no ice cream the rest of their lives if they didn't behave. She'd made King promise to leave most of the talking to her. She'd *insisted* Mitch stay in the background until her parents were gone.

At the top of the stairs, she let herself breathe again. Her children sat on the couch, squirming and fidgeting like a lineup of little rascals—but sitting. Still clean. Not fighting. Miracles could happen! Ellie's heart swelled with love.

"Mom, Dad, these are your grandchildren—Gabe, Michael, Rafe and Seri. And their friend, Bubba Sue. Say hello to your grandma and grandpa."

"Hello," they chorused uncomfortably, then fell solemnly quiet.

Ellie's mother hurried to the sofa. "I'm so glad to see you. Gordon, please bring the bag." She sat down beside Seri and took her hand. "Seri? That's such a beautiful name."

"It's Seraphina, really," Seri said quietly, holding her hand very still. "It means angel."

"That's lovely."

The children sat ominously silent.

Ellie's father set the bag down, then wandered around the room examining everything. "And what kind of a name is Rafe?"

A perfectly good name. Ellie felt her tension mount, but she bit back the retort. Her children were being *too* quiet. Why couldn't her father question *that,* or fuss about the dust she'd missed on the TV screen? Or Bubba Sue's name!

Spotting Mitch's Winterhaven jacket on the back of a chair, her father sauntered over. "Who did you say you were living with here, Ellen?" He seemed to eye the jacket for size. "*Another* musician?"

Her children squirmed, and the tension in the room shot up by degrees. Her father was making clear he wasn't ready to forgive and forget.

"I suppose he's out on a—what do you call them?"

"They're called a gig," a familiar voice answered.

Ellie's heartbeat stumbled. From the doorway leading to the kitchen, a foot appeared—dressed in a red sock, attached to a leg in a cast, extending from a wheelchair, followed by the rest of King—and then Mitch, wheeling him into the room.

"But King isn't in any shape to handle that kind of activity nowadays," Mitch added.

She shouldn't be so glad to see them, but all she could do was gaze at them in mute gratitude.

King looked almost debonair in his red socks. In the last week and a half, since he'd been helping Mitch prepare for the concert, he'd begun to look really healthy. And Mitch? All she could think was that he looked solid and respectable and stable...and gorgeous. Dressed up for company. His white shirt shone like snow, the cuffs rolled halfway up his arms, and his gray slacks held a crisp crease. The very sight of him still made her breathless.

"Mom... Dad, this is—"

"Kendall Kole, proprietor of the King Kole Music Shoppe downstairs." King held out his hand to Ellie's father. "Call me King."

Gordon Whittaker stalked over and shook hands

stiffly. His impenetrable gaze moved from King to Mitch. Then to Ellie.

Almost unconsciously, she raised her chin.

King winked at her. "I'd shake your lovely mother's hand, too, but I don't get around much anymore." He patted the cast on his outstretched leg, as if to reassure her parents he was harmless.

But Mitch wasn't harmless; she could see it written all over her father's face. As far as Gordon Whittaker was concerned, he'd just met the big bad wolf. And he was still trying to be protective and overbearing. He certainly had her children subdued.

But she was a grown woman now. She had to show him he didn't need to treat her that way anymore.

"Dad, this is Mitch Kole, King's son. He's here from Colorado to—"

"*He's* The Prince," Seri announced solemnly. "He takes care of King."

That was all the other kids needed. Michael stifled giggles. Rafe pounced on Gabe to keep him from smothering Seri. The dog barked. The sofa springs shrieked.

And Ellie's hopes fled. Her father had little patience with undisciplined children. None for fairy tales.

Casting a pleading glance at her kids, she turned back to Mitch. "Mitch, my parents, Carolyn and Gordon Whittaker."

Mitch shook their hands. "Clever granddaughter you've got there, Mr. Whittaker. Makes those associations fast. Matter of fact, they're all bright. And good-natured. A little nervous right *now*, but you're going to be very proud of them."

The charm fairly spun out of him, but Ellie couldn't get mad. All she could think was that Mitch had come to her rescue. The Prince had shown up to shield her from the dragon's fire—that was what Seri would say.

Peter had never done that. In all their time together, he'd never faced the dragon for her. He'd never been willing to make amends with her father.

"So *why* are you living here, Ellie?"

Her father's question jolted her back to the present. Mitch might have rescued her temporarily, but *she* had to face her father sometime. This was the life she'd chosen, and it was far from a fairy tale. If her father still disapproved, she would have to come to terms with that—without Mitch's charm. Without her old dreams and storybook illusions. Her life was based on reality now.

"Dad, I told you in my letter. King offered me and the kids a place to stay until I can get—"

"Ellie is a big help to me," King interrupted.

Mitch wheeled King farther into the room.

Ellie pulled a chair in from the dining table to sit down on. "Mitch, don't you and King have something to—"

"Thanks, Ellie." He took the chair from her and set it next to Ellie's mother. Then he sat down on it himself! "King can tell you, Mr. and Mrs. Whittaker, Ellie is pretty amazing."

"Wait! Mitch...?" She tried to get his attention, but he'd focused all that masculine energy on her mother.

"She takes care of your grandkids, runs the store, goes to school..."

Ellie shook her head furtively, but he refused to see.

"...and then when King was injured, she insisted on caring for him, too. Your daughter is quite a woman." At last, he turned to look at her.

Darned if she hadn't wished for the wrong thing again.

Because he smiled—one of those slow, persuasive kinds of smiles that made her knees go weak, made her forget to breathe. What was worse, he looked as if he meant every word of it.

Ellie grew light-headed. He was carrying this too far. She and her kids were just barely making it. Her parents would never believe their rebellious daughter had become a candidate for sainthood. Her father would do another one of his rejection numbers, and her children would never get to know their grandparents.

"Course, the kids help out, too," King chimed in. "Gabe's doing great in the store. Becoming quite a salesman, I understand."

"Gabe can sell?" It was the first spark of interest Gordon Whittaker had shown in his grandchildren.

Mitch nodded. "Does a great job. And Michael has the energy of a Wall Street floor trader. Now, Rafe…he may have a future in telemarketing."

Ellie choked on a laugh. She must be getting hysterical.

"As for The Princess—" Mitch reached over to tug one of Seri's curls "—she's a great storyteller."

Seri beamed.

Ellie's mother beamed, too. "Ellie, I'm so proud of you. And your children." Her attention swung back to the handsome young man beside her, and she actually began to glow.

Her poor mother. In less time than it took to say abracadabra, Carolyn Whittaker had become absolutely smitten with Mitch. And Seri was in the same condition. Did things like that run in families?

Suddenly Mitch was up and holding the back of his chair. "Here, Ellie, sit by your mother. It's time for King's therapy." He stepped behind King's wheelchair.

She should have known. Mitch didn't mind creating illusions with *her* story, but when the plot looked as if *he* might be getting more involved, he was ready to run.

"Don't you remember, Mitch?" She smiled daggers at him. "The doctor said it would do King good to be around people."

He fumbled with the wheelchair brake.

"Why don't you stay and visit?" she taunted. "Mrs. Givens can run him through his therapy while we're at the concert." *Let's see how you wiggle out of this, Mr. Charmer.*

"I know, stay for dinner!" Carolyn Whittaker bubbled. "We'll make it a party. I'm sure we can order pizza from somewhere."

"Yes!" The kids bounced up from the squeaking sofa.

Mitch looked stricken.

Ellie went numb. Her parents didn't understand about Mitch. Her father would probably disown her all over again. But she had to tell them. She had to be up-front and honest from now on. She just prayed that would be good enough.

"Mom, Mitch is staying *here*. He has a bed in the same room with King—to help him at night." She checked her father's reaction. He was frowning.

Mitch stepped forward. "It was my idea, Mr. Whittaker. In fact, I insisted on it. Ellie couldn't handle King by herself. But I wouldn't want you to get the wrong impression...what with Ellie being a single mother and me being a man and—" He stumbled to a halt. His tan turned a ruddy shade of rust.

Almost as if against his will, he sought Ellie's gaze. "I mean, your daughter is a lovely woman—" his eyes shaded with meaning ''—but I can assure you, she is a model of decorum.''

A model of decorum? Once again The Prince had charged to her rescue, even if he had stumbled a little. Ellie wanted to laugh—to keep herself from crying. Because Mitch's careful words stirred a rush of regret.

''Well.'' Gordon Whittaker cleared his throat. ''I see.'' He looked from Ellie to Mitch and then at King. ''I...guess I owe both of you my thanks.'' He glanced at Ellie, couldn't hold her gaze. ''For being such gentlemen. For giving Ellie this...opportunity. She always was one to go after what she wanted.

''Her mother says she's like me in that,'' he added quietly.

Tears filled Ellie's eyes. This might be as close to forgiveness as her father would ever get. She couldn't let it pass unacknowledged. Crossing the room, she held out her arms for a hug. ''Thanks for taking me back, Dad.''

He cleared his throat again. ''I'm glad you finally asked us, honey.'' This time his hug was warm and enfolding.

Ellie laughed as she brushed tears from his sports coat. ''Mitch was the one who insisted I write.'' Stepping back, she sought Mitch's gaze, to tell him with her tears what she couldn't say in words. To thank him for badgering her and pushing her into contacting her parents. Mitch had made this reconciliation possible.

But Mitch didn't seem to notice. Already he'd turned back to her mother.

Ellie swept away the remnants of her tears. Just one more woman whose heart he'd steal...before he went away.

* * *

Mitch zigzagged through the crowd, dodging scuffling kids, skirting families folding lawn chairs, avoiding grandmas pushing baby strollers across the stretches of grass. Glancing back, he made sure he traveled away from Ellie and her parents where they stood under a spotlight near the stage.

He'd told them he would meet them at the flat after the concert, that he wanted to get back to check on King. The truth was, he couldn't let himself be drawn any further into Ellie's life.

With fumbling fingers, he loosened the tie King had loaned him, flicked open his top shirt button. Exhaled with a rush.

Thank goodness the visit was almost over. Carolyn Whittaker's gifts had loosened her grandkids' tongues. Her pizza party had been a noisy success. Even stiff old Gordon had relaxed a little after Ellie's hug. He'd even managed to smile.

At the crest of a grassy incline, Mitch looked back in time to see the four kids elbow their way through to Ellie and her parents. He watched Carolyn Whittaker pat them shyly on the shoulder. Almost chuckled when Gordon shook Gabe's hand! Could imagine Ellie's laughter as she wrapped them all in a family hug.

The gesture tightened a knot in his stomach. He was snooping, watching a scene in which he didn't belong. Just like this afternoon. A family scene was something he wanted no part of. Yanking the tie from his neck, he wrapped it around his fist and strode away.

Ellie was reconciling with her parents, just as he'd hoped would happen. King was recuperating. Soon they could all get on with their lives, and Mitch could get back to his. That was what he wanted.

Right. Like a kid in a candy store wanted to be somewhere else.

Damn it, he wanted Ellie. But she wasn't the kind of woman a man could have without strings. Without commitments.

And Mitch Kole didn't make family kinds of commitments.

Besides, he didn't deserve a woman as fine as Ellie— any more than King had deserved his mother. He would never make the mistake his father had.

Footsteps thundered down the hall. The walls rang with shouts and barking. Like a litter of gangly puppies, the four Sander kids and Bubba Sue tumbled into the dormitory and raced to the side of King's hospital bed. Carolyn and Gordon Whittaker followed close behind.

King leaned forward eagerly. "So how was it?"

Mitch shoved another pillow behind his father and plumped up the whole pile. Keeping busy meant he wouldn't be able to watch for Ellie, which was fine, because her opinion of the kids' performance didn't matter to him. The fact that Ellie hadn't come in with the rest of her family didn't bother him at all.

"It was awesome!" Michael proclaimed.

Mitch squared the blanket across King's casts and ignored a flicker of satisfaction.

"Excellent," Gabe pronounced.

Frowning, Mitch bent to check the switches that raised and lowered the bed.

"Mitch was the best."

He straightened and caught Seri's gaze. She gazed at him adoringly. Not to be outdone, Rafe stepped forward. "Guess he learned it from you, King."

Mitch swiped a hand back through his hair and

squelched a growl. He was a fool to be so pleased at the kids' words.

Carolyn Whittaker stepped between Michael and Gabe, resting a possessive hand on each of their shoulders. "They were absolutely fantastic!"

They could have sung a funeral dirge in Swahili and Carolyn Whittaker would have loved it, Mitch brooded. This was one happy grandmother. But Ellie's father had his wife beat hands down. Gordon Whittaker stood behind the two younger Sander kids with Seri's big pink rabbit lodged under one arm. The Princess had won another subject.

Mitch did a double take. In Gordon's other hand, he carried the portable telephone!

Ellie's heart-wounded, ragamuffin kids had won their grandfather over. If Gordon Whittaker could bend, then happy endings could happen after all.

Mitch's gaze swung to the doorway—he couldn't help himself. He'd known the moment Ellie came in.

Sweet Ellie, so pretty even in that old denim skirt and baggy blue sweater; so saucy and seductive, even with her proud chin and sparking eyes. And too damned realistic, he reminded himself. This was the woman who had gone cold turkey on fairy tales. But with evidence like this, how could she not believe in happy endings now?

"So what do *you* think, Ellie?" Damn, he hadn't meant to ask. He didn't want her opinion to matter.

Slowly she met his gaze. "The kids were wonderful." Her eyes glistened. "You were wonderful."

Suddenly the floor seemed to shift beneath his feet.

"By God, I *knew* they'd sing well!" King bellowed, setting the bed to rocking. "I'm so proud of you." His beaming smile seemed to include everyone in the room. Especially Mitch.

After their first performance, Mitch had expected to feel relieved. Maybe a little self-righteous about filling in for his father. But not proud. Not gratified.

"Wish I could have been there," King added quietly. Not humbled.

"I wish you could have, too...Dad."

The room grew uncomfortably quiet—except for Ellie's quick intake of air. He couldn't look at her again.

"Thanks, son. That means a lot."

"Yeah, well..."

Independent, self-reliant, cool Mitchell Kole waxing emotional? What was happening to him?

He punched King's pillows. "Time for you to get some sleep. Everybody out."

"Now hold on a second here, son. I'm not ready to—"

Carolyn Whittaker put her hand on Mitch's arm. "The kids are bursting to tell your father all about the concert. Don't you think this one night...? Especially now that he's practically one of the family."

"No!"

Everyone turned to stare at him. Which was fine...because it made him feel more like himself. More like a heel. Heels didn't get envious of other people's families.

"It's late," he growled. "King needs his rest."

"Come on, Mitch, this kind of break in his routine will be good for him."

Ellie's appealing eyes all but did him in.

"Speaking of breaks..."

Carolyn Whittaker looked up at him, and he discovered just where Ellie got her devastating smile.

"I'd guess you and Ellie don't get many breaks around here. It's such a beautiful evening. While we're here to baby-sit, why don't the two of you go and enjoy the festivities."

Chapter Seven

Mitch strode along the sidewalk beside Ellie. At least he tried. But somehow Ellie managed to keep several feet between them. She'd avoided him ever since they'd left the flat.

He didn't know what to do with the magnetism that played between them. Which was why he never should have gone along with the Whittakers' suggestion to come out into this silvery evening with their daughter.

Their divorced, single-parent-of-four-kids, in-need-of-a-husband daughter. He needed some hard-nosed reminders like that right now. He needed to talk to someone who understood him. But he was pretty sure a phone call to Jack wouldn't do a damn bit of good. Mitch would have to tell him that wherever he went, whatever he was doing, he was always aware of Ellie. She could be walking a block away and he'd still feel her presence. She drew him—like a big dumb bumblebee to a sweet, bright flower.

And Jack would listen with that perceptive silence of

his and say, *Just the power of honey, Mitch. I knew it would strike someday.*

Mitch didn't need to hear *that*.

He glanced at his watch. Okay, one hour. That was all he'd give it. Long enough to convince Ellie's parents that he and Ellie had done the KirkKnoll Days thing. But not long enough for them to consider him potential family material. They might open their arms to King, but, Mitch reminded himself, *he* didn't make family kinds of commitments. He didn't need them.

"So where do you want to go?" he mumbled.

"Nowhere in particular. It's just nice to walk."

Wrong. With Ellie, walking could be dangerous. He shoved both hands deep into his pockets and did his best to shorten his stride. Her faint, fresh fragrance played between them. He moved a little nearer.

Ellie sidestepped, putting space between them again.

"You were lucky, you know," she said quickly. "Growing up here—in the middle of everything."

He exhaled a blunt laugh. "A flat over a store isn't exactly a castle, Ellie. Even if Seri thinks so."

Ellie glanced at him, her brows arching quizzically. "But it's in such a nice little town." A wistful smile played around her mouth.

Tempting him. Like honey. He had to look away.

"Nice little town?" After his mother's death, it had felt more like a prison. He'd spent too many nights roaming these same dark streets, too much time hanging out at the old stone train station yearning to jump a boxcar.

"My kids like it."

Mitch glanced around. "I'd forgotten there was so much street activity." Families out on warm spring evenings like tonight, their kids' mouths stuffed with cotton candy, their babies sacked out in strollers.

Being with Ellie almost made his memories just what they ought to be—things of the past.

"I guess it's okay." But not a place he'd choose to stay in. Not a place *he'd* ever call home again.

"Just okay?" That rare humor danced in her eyes. "Come on, Mitch, where else can you play in the park, buy a fresh-baked chocolate-chip cookie *and* a bubble gum cigar—" she ticked off the items on her slender fingers "—sample a free strawberry at the farmers' market and walk home, all in an afternoon? Where else could I feel safe letting my kids do that on their own?"

"In Winterhaven." The words were out of his mouth before he realized what they implied. "In Winterhaven," he rushed on, "folks do all that *and* drink cappuccino at the outdoor café, buy cut flowers at the corner stand..." He reached for her still-raised hand to count off his own points on her fingers. Her wrist felt almost feverish; her fingers shook a little. As they had when he'd captured her thimble.

"They ride horses all summer and ski all winter," he stumbled on, kicking himself for having started this, "...in the most magnificent mountains you can imagine. People are *crazy* about the place."

Abruptly Ellie withdrew her hand. She angled away, putting more distance between them than before.

He was crazy. Playing finger footsy with this irresistible woman was crazy. *It has finally happened,* Jack would pronounce if he saw him now—Mitch Kole, avowed bachelor, devoted free spirit, acting like some greenhorn adolescent. Trying to trick Ellie into holding hands.

"Look, let's just walk to the park and back and call

it a night, okay?'' Before he did something they would both regret.

Ellie picked up the pace. ''Good idea.''

Darn. If it was such a great idea, why did she suddenly have to force herself to hurry? She was making a big mistake being out here with Mitch on a romantic night like this. After such a happy day, she shouldn't be courting disaster with a man who couldn't wait to get back to his mountains. A shiver crept up her back.

Mitch lengthened his stride to match hers. ''Cold?''

She listened to their footsteps scuff in unison on the sidewalk. If she could just make it to the park and back without yielding to his nearness.

''Not really cold,'' she answered. She didn't want him offering her his jacket. Didn't want him invading her reality zone. But he'd already done that a long time ago.

''A little scared, maybe.''

''Why scared?''

She could tell he'd turned to look at her, but she focused straight ahead. ''Because my kids did so well with the show. Because my parents are back in my life.'' She drew in a long breath. ''Because things seem to be going so much better between you and your father.'' Too much like a fairy tale. She didn't believe in happy endings.

''I misjudged you, Mitch. I didn't think you really wanted to help. But everything good today you made happen.'' Yet he was still going away.

Mitch huffed softly. The sound sent the shivers skittering across her shoulders. She didn't dare look at him. If he smiled, she was scared her willpower would disappear.

''Ellie, everything that happened today was because of *you*.''

He sounded impatient, but she didn't care. She wanted

him to tell her he'd *chosen* to become involved—even if only for this short time.

"*I* wasn't the one who insisted my parents be invited—"

"*Somebody* had to get you to stop being so damned proud. You and your kids *need* an extended family. Besides, it was pretty obvious your father was just looking for an opportunity to make up." Mitch sounded almost angry.

His denial sent the shivers racing down her back. She straightened her shoulders. "Okay, what about King?" she challenged. "You can't deny you and he became a lot closer working together on the—"

"Ellie, I didn't know the first thing about teaching kids to sing. Besides, it helped pass the time."

She'd expected resistance, but tonight Mitch's words were less sharp than usual. Something to hang hope on.

"All I know is you're a good son. You made him very happy. And proud."

Her words were met with silence.

Mitch's stride lengthened. Darkness hid all but his angular silhouette, making him look massive and dangerous.

But she'd come too far to turn back now. "Mitch? I can't help wondering what happened between you and—"

He fairly growled. "That's not the kind of story you'd be interested in."

"Okay, then let's talk about a different kind of story. Mitch Kole and the Sander kids."

"Your kids did great because they've had training. Because they had family in the audience."

She could feel him glaring at her. All the things she'd known about him from the beginning came rushing back, sending a different kind of quaking down her back.

Mitch was rejecting credit for everything. Refusing to acknowledge responsibility. But she wouldn't let him get away with it this time.

"My kids did well because you spent time with them. You helped them instead of driving them. You *cared* about them, Mitch. You'd make a good father!" She flung the words at him like an accusation. Tears sprang to her eyes.

"I would *not* make a good father. I don't even *like*—"

From out of the darkness, a rumble overrode his harsh words. A pack of teenagers hurtled around the corner, their in-line skates roaring on the sidewalk. The leader sliced between them, throwing Ellie off balance. She teetered backward.

"Ellie!" Mitch reached for her, but two more skaters cut through, arms flailing.

"Hey, watch where you're—"

They raced past, sending Ellie careening against the building. The rest surged by in a blur, disappearing like thunder down the shadowed sidewalk.

Mitch caught her by the shoulders. His eyes were dark with concern. "Are you all right?"

His hands felt strong and protective, but she wasn't all right at all. Her heart thundered, and she could barely breathe. Her knees felt as if they'd give way, and she wanted to melt against him just to soothe his anger, just to—

She shook herself. "I'm fine." But she never should have looked up. His dark eyes searched hers, held her mesmerized. She couldn't keep from looking to his mouth, drawn tight with outrage and worry.

Slowly, as if by sheer force of will, he loosened his grip on her shoulders. "You're not hurt?"

She waited, breathless, watching the struggle in his eyes. Then she turned her face up to him.

His hands drifted down her arms, sending sweet ribbons of heat swirling through her. His fingers sought hers hesitantly, until he laced them through hers and held her fast.

She could feel him trying to resist. She could sense the conflict that poured off him, the same struggle that raged inside her. She shouldn't have started this. She should stop it now, before it was too late. But she couldn't make herself pull away.

How many years had it been since a man had simply held her hands? When had it ever felt like this? Mitch's touch made her feverish. Made her want him. His touch made her melt inside. How could something so innocent be so...sensual?

This wasn't like any fairy tale she'd ever read. No self-respecting fair maiden ever got the hots for The Prince. But tonight...

Barely able to breathe, she rose on tiptoes. Just one kiss...just magic for one night. That was all Cinderella had asked.

Then his mouth brushed hers, softly, almost reluctantly, filling her with hunger and urgency. She leaned into him to close the gap, and his uncertainty seemed to flee. His arms swept around her, encircling her in warmth and strength, drawing her against the lean, hard length of him. His solidness made her yield, filled her with the sweet languor of wanting. His mouth closed over hers, and she slid her arms around his neck to draw tighter against him, to feel every inch of him, to absorb his heat.

As if a spell were unwinding, he kissed her, hard and bruising, molding his mouth to hers, seeking entry to deepen the kiss. Like a sorcerer, he made her forget everything but him; like a wizard, he filled her with magic. But Mitch was a man, every hard, burning inch of him pressing against her.

She kissed him back, opening to his urgency, trembling at the quaking she felt in him. She savored his taste, she breathed in the faint, crisp scent of pine mingled with his own musky heat, she felt the thunder of his heart against her own.

Or was it the galloping race of time? For an instant, she listened, knowing tonight the only things she and Cinderella had in common were a prince and a fatefully ticking clock. In a few days, Ellie Sander's prince would be gone.

But in this story, she'd known all along he was going. She just hadn't realized what he would leave behind. Not kids and broken promises, not even a shiny glass slipper. Just a foolish, incurable dreamer...who had gone and fallen in love.

Mitch couldn't get enough of Ellie. As if she'd cast some kind of spell, all his desire, all his fantasies, the ones he thought he'd stuffed away, swept over him. They made him forget everything but this little bit of a woman whose feathery blond head reached no higher than his chin.

He pulled her closer, all but lifting her from her feet. Heaven help him, there was no saving him now, because she melted against him, her lush body fitting to his as if they'd been designed to be together. He kissed her again and again, his mouth devouring her, her lips at first soft and yielding, then hungry and seeking. She tasted sweet, like cotton candy; she smelled fresh like the outdoors. The soft murmurs in her throat fueled his urgency. She filled up his senses, made him want her more than any woman he'd ever known.

How could this be happening to him? How could he be feeling this insatiable need for her?

She nibbled his lower lip, shafting incandescence through him, then pulled a little away as if to catch her breath. Under his hands, her movements taunted his fingers; her soft sweater felt like velvet covering bare, inviting skin.

Holding his face, she pulled him into another kiss, her mouth opening to his. She was too luscious. Too desirable.

With his hands, he measured the curve of her slender waist, traced upward along her trim midriff, brushed the hard peaks of her full breasts as he found the front of her blouse. He fumbled with the buttons.

She drew in a sharp, trembling breath.

"Ellie." He heard her name in a whisper and realized the voice was his own. At the sound, he stopped.

What was he doing?

This *was* Ellie, not some pet-food heiress looking for a romp in the snow with the local ski stud. Ellie—who deserved a hell of a lot more than a little groping on a neighborhood street corner. Ellie…who had four kids. He didn't even *like* kids. That was what he'd been going to tell her. It was what he *needed* to believe.

"Mitch?" Her voice sounded very young. Very scared.

He kissed her gently, nipping the edges of her lips. "It's okay, Ellie," he whispered, tasting her sweetness one last time, trying to file it away for future memories.

He eased her back until she looked up at him, searching his face with tremulous hope. Gently he reached down and took her hand. "Come on, Ellie. It's time to go."

She held his gaze for a long time, her passion ebbing to the most devastating sadness he'd ever seen.

At last, almost imperceptibly, her chin rose. For an instant, starlight glittered from the moisture in her eyes. She reached up and pressed her lips to his cheek, more tenderly than he'd ever been kissed.

Then she pulled her hand from his. "I'm ready."

Such a simple thing, but it felt like surgery without anesthesia. As if his heart had just been torn away.

Chapter Eight

"Are you ready?" Ellie whispered.

Six heads seesawed up and down. One short, black tail whipped back and forth.

From the far side of the kitchen counter, Ellie eyed the lineup before her. Michael hopped from one foot to the other, wrestling his T-shirt off over his head. Beside him, Gabe stood at attention, his blond curls uncombed, his feet bare, his high-tops tied together and slung over his shoulder. Seri in her tutu and Rafe in his oversize sleeping shirt flanked King where he sat, dog in lap, just the other side of the kitchen door. Behind him, Harriet Givens gripped his wheelchair handles like an Olympic racer poised for the starting gun.

Poor Bubba Sue. If King petted her any harder, the dog would go bald. *Poor King.* Ellie couldn't blame him for being nervous. So was she. But that didn't stop her from giving in to a mushy smile. They were all taking this so seriously. She just hoped they could carry off her deception. Before Mitch left, she owed him this for all he'd done for them. Even if he wouldn't accept credit for it.

In the store below, a door slammed.

Everybody stood as still as statues.

Footsteps started up the back stairs.

"You know what to do," she whispered.

The words were scarcely out of her mouth before the lineup scattered. Michael and Gabe skimmed down the hall to the dormitory. Seri and Rafe pranced after them, somehow managing to keep from tripping over Bubba Sue. Harriet whirled King in front of the TV, then disappeared in the opposite direction.

Ellie couldn't believe they were capable of such quiet.

The top of Mitch's head appeared through the stair railing. The rest of him ascended into view—rugged face taut with intention, a shock of dark hair falling over his forehead, damp curls breaching the collar of his crisp white shirt, pleated gray slacks riding snug and low on his hips.

Ellie's breath caught in her throat. He looked formidable. He looked stunning. In spite of everything, or because of it, he could still make her breathless.

He paused on the landing, pulled a handkerchief from his pocket and blotted his forehead. "Boxes are broken down like you wanted." He avoided looking at her. "I put them out by the trash. Anything else you need done?" He concentrated on refolding the handkerchief.

Ellie struggled between relief and dismay. Mitch had stayed out of her way all day—which had helped a lot when it came to making preparations. But she knew that hadn't been the reason. He'd denied responsibility for everything else last night. She supposed he was denying their kisses, too. Trying to make her think their kisses hadn't meant anything more to him than just…kisses.

Kind of like dessert—tempting and sweet, but not something to indulge in on a regular basis. She didn't believe *that*, either.

"No…" She cleared the feathers from her throat and raised her chin. "Nothing more to do. But I'm…not sure the kids are ready. Maybe you'd better go on to the park alone. We'll be along…as soon as Harriet gets here."

His frown deepened. "Not ready?" Cutting a wide path around her, he strode down the hall. "Hey, gang, time to go. Everybody front and center."

Ellie held her breath. This just had to work.

Seri stepped into the hall from the Mermaid Room, her tutu straps dangling from slumped shoulders, her chin drooping. "I can't find my rabbit," she said sadly.

Michael popped out of the dormitory in his skivvies. "Is it time *already*?"

"Mom, where's my white shirt?" Rafe chimed in.

Crossing her fingers, Ellie marched down the hall to block Mitch's progress. "I *thought* they might not be ready."

Gabe stuck his head out of the bathroom. "I'm not going," he grumbled, his face scrunched into a major pout.

"Oh dear." Ellie looked up at Mitch imploringly, which wasn't too difficult under the circumstances. Except she had to remember that what she was about to implore him to do didn't involve kissing.

"Please, Mitch, just go on." She moved toward him, fairly certain he'd back away. The closer she came, the faster he retreated. Darn him. She wanted him to leave, but he didn't have to scramble!

"Are you sure, Ellie?" He sidestepped toward the kitchen. "I can wait."

"But the rest of the kids will be looking for you."

She pressed forward, driving him back into the kitchen. "They'll be worried and upset if you're not there." With grim determination, she herded him into the main room.

King barely looked up from the TV. "See you after the concert, son."

Ellie gathered the jacket and tie draped over the front railing and handed them to Mitch. She mustered a smile, forced herself to look up at him.

Which made her heart all but stop. Mitch held her gaze, his eyes dark blue, one corner of his mouth tugged sideways in a sad imitation of a smile. Slowly his gaze slid to her lips.

All her good sense crumbled. She leaned nearer, raised her face. Her eyes drifted closed...and popped open again as he thumped down the stairs and slammed the door behind him.

She let out a slow breath. Swallowed back the lump in her throat. Blinked the moisture from her eyes. How could she bear to see this man go out of her life for good?

"Is he gone?" Gabe hollered.

Soon Mitch *would* be gone—he was that kind of man. Not the kind she was supposed to fall in love with.

But she'd have plenty of time for regrets later.

"Yes, he's gone. Let's get moving!"

Seri and Rafe raced in with armloads of pillows and dumped them on the sofa. Gabe and Michael thundered down the back stairs, then pounded back up dragging flattened cardboard boxes that *thunked* against every last spoke of the railing.

Harriet marched into the room and crossed to the top of the front stairs. "Bring that cardboard over here, boys."

From behind him, King pulled out a neatly folded shirt. "Hope I didn't wrinkle this too much."

Ellie helped him slide out of his T-shirt and into the crisp new sport shirt. Its aquamarine print made his eyes almost as blue as Mitch's. She had to look away.

Dragging the coffee table nearer, Seri climbed on top. "I'll comb King's hair."

"I've got the flowers," Rafe announced, holding up a bulging plastic grocery bag.

Harriet peered down the stairwell at Gabe and Michael. "Overlap those edges, boys. Tape them together good. Don't be stingy now. That's what duct tape is for. Make sure those sides are wedged in tight against the walls. We want that cardboard to stay put."

At last she pronounced the structure acceptable. "Let's get King hooked up."

Ellie wheeled King to the top of the stairs and set the brake firmly. She handed Harriet the harness Mitch had devised to hoist King up that first day home from the hospital. Deftly Harriet strapped him in and connected him to the ropes.

Ellie followed every move, double-checked every clip. They were taking such a risk. What if they couldn't hold King? What if he'd lost too much strength in his arms to help? They were endangering his limbs for sure. Maybe even his life.

She shuddered.

But Harriet had assessed King's condition. She'd reviewed Ellie's plan. She'd declared them compatible. She'd even offered to help. Ellie just prayed everything went all right.

"What do you think, King?" Her fingers trembled as she strapped pillows around his casts with bungee cords.

King shoved himself forward in his seat. "I think we should get this show on the road."

"Okay! Let's have a look at everybody," Harriet commanded. "White shirts, navy shorts...good. Michael, zip your fly. Gabe, tuck your shirttail in. Rafe, no phone. Seri, let's see you smile. Okay! Everyone to their positions. Prepare to lower the King!"

Ellie's heart raced. This just had to succeed. Mitch's intervention had worked magic between her and her parents. Maybe she could ply a little magic, too—to help heal whatever hurt festered between Mitch and his father. She wanted to do this for them both before Mitch left. Because she didn't have enough magic to make a man like him stay.

Mitch glanced down at the twelve kids sprawled at his feet on the grass at KirkKnoll Park. Their worried eyes moved slowly from side to side. Damn, he was pacing again.

He stopped and checked his watch. Listened to the applause as the Tap Kats dancers took their third bow on the other side of the amphitheater shell.

One more act before theirs. They'd have to perform without Ellie's kids.

Mitch tried to ignore a wave of disappointment.

"Okay, gang, everybody line up. We're on after the Beauty Shop Quartet."

A little girl in pigtails tugged his pant leg. "What about Gabe?"

"Yeah, where's Michael and those other guys?" the rest of the kids chorused.

That was what Mitch wanted to know. Ellie had been against their performing from the start, yet she'd agreed to let them sing for King's benefit. Now that King was better, now that her parents had come and gone, she'd probably thought better of it again.

Performing without the Sander kids would feel... empty.

"I think maybe they...had to be somewhere else." More likely, anywhere *he* wasn't. Because Ellie still didn't trust him, even after last night.

Especially after last night.

Last night...Ellie in his arms, Ellie's breath mingling with his, Ellie's lips, her sweet, moist kisses, her body folding into his—

"Mr. Kole, I'm scared." The little girl chewed the end of a pigtail.

So am I, kiddo, so am I. He'd been scared ever since the first time he'd laid eyes on Ellie. Ever since last night. He wasn't supposed to feel like this. Not about any woman. Not about Ellie.

Mitch leaned down and tickled the little kid's nose with her other pigtail. "Don't worry, munchkin. You'll do just fine."

He, on the other hand, was not doing fine at all. Damn, where had Jack been last night? Just because Mitch had called at two in the morning was no excuse for Jack not to answer.

Mitch had had to wrestle with the questions by himself. Turned out he didn't need Jack to tell him what he already knew—that Ellie was one incredible woman. That she deserved nothing less than a prince. That not even her best intentions could turn *him* into that prince.

Mitch should just forget his disappointment. He should be glad she and her kids weren't here.

"Hey, Mr. Kole, look!"

Across the wide expanse of lawn, four kids raced toward them waving their arms.

Ellie's kids! They'd fled the castle. They'd come to perform…in the name of the King.

He waved back, beckoning them to hurry, feeling suddenly as anxious and fidgety as the kids bouncing around him.

And they might as well send for the men with the nets, because he was obviously losing it. Standing here in the middle of a neighborhood park pretending this was a fairy tale. Feeling as elated as a kid checking off who had come to his birthday party. It shouldn't make a bit of difference to him if Ellie's kids were here or not. But it did.

Michael dashed up with Rafe close on his heels. Gabe trotted behind Seri, bringing up the rear. Miraculously, Gabe was smiling. "We made it," he announced between puffs.

"I'm glad you're here." To Mitch's amazement, he really meant it.

"Prince!" Seri threw her arms around his knees, almost taking him down.

Damn! For a princess, Seri sure knew how to tackle. What was worse, he loved her for it.

He leaned down, resisting the inclination to swing her up in a hug. Instead he peeled her arms from his legs. "Where's your mommy?" he whispered.

Suddenly she was backing out of his hands, frowning up at him with her big, brown eyes. "I don't know."

She didn't know? Or was she just avoiding telling him Ellie wasn't coming?

"It's okay, Seri. Look…" He pulled a small tape recorder from his pocket. It was a plan he and King had decided on that afternoon. "We'll tape your singing so your mom can—"

Applause overrode his words. A shot of adrenaline pumped through him.

"Okay, gang, we're on. You're gonna do great."

Mitch led the kids around the amphitheater shell and up onto the stage. Striding to the center, he faced them, trying to calm their nervousness with a reassuring smile. Allowing himself a brief swell of pride. A chance to get used to this rush of new feelings.

Actually they were great kids. With King's help, he'd managed to encourage some pretty good talent out of them. They'd make their last performance the best, something Ellie would cherish for years. He wanted to leave *something* behind with her that was good. Something good from *him*.

Pulling the tape player from his pocket, he set it to record and laid it on the music stand. Then he raised a hand for attention.

The kids began to giggle.

He touched a silencing finger to his lips.

The giggles increased.

He frowned.

A smattering of applause rippled through the audience, and the kids' hands flew to their mouths. They wiggled with muffled laughter.

What was going on?

"Look, Prince," Seri whispered, pointing behind him.

He eyed her dubiously, then turned.

From the shadows of the center aisle, a figure emerged. It seemed to float toward the stage—with one leg extended in front like a battering ram, and a foot covered by a red sock. King! Riding what looked like a flower-decorated throne. Smiling broader than Mitch had ever seen him smile.

How in the world?

In the warm glow of the stage lights, Mitch caught sight of Ellie behind King's chair. She slowed the flowery throne to a stop at the first row and sat down in an empty space…next to Harriet Givens!

Unbelievable! Ellie hadn't pulled the kids out of the show after all. Instead this incredible little woman had managed to get King all the way here, broken bones, double casts and grumpy disposition be damned. If anyone could do it, Ellie could.

Mitch couldn't begin to imagine how. But he knew why. Stepping forward, he raised his hands for quiet.

"Ladies and gentlemen. Neighbors. Tonight King Kole's Kids will perform in recognition of their founder and teacher, Kendall 'King' Kole. In spite of multiple broken bones, he's here tonight to hear them sing."

A spattering of applause broke out, but at the sight of King's proud smile, Mitch held up his hand. Before the old defenses could set in, he let himself go with the new feelings that overwhelmed him this evening.

"King is also my father, and I just want to say…thanks, Dad, for all your help."

Applause swept through the audience. Mitch stepped out of the spotlight, and the white circle slid from the stage to King, who smiled and waved as Ellie turned his chair to face the crowd. To Mitch's surprise, the clapping increased.

But it faded from Mitch's awareness as he looked to Ellie. Her honey brown hair brushed her creamy white shoulders, shoulders that were bare except for straps of a pretty blue dress that hugged her luscious curves and swayed softly around a shapely pair of legs.

Ellie was wearing a dress! She looked about as pretty as a woman should be allowed to look.

Turning, she gazed up at him. Her eyes sparkled.

Brushing fingertips across her cheeks, she said something to him, shaping the words with her full, rosy lips.

Thank you.

Mitch wanted to leap from the stage and sweep her into his arms. Instead he spoke quietly into the microphone, offering her the best he had to give.

"This is for you, Ellie."

The applause faded, and he turned to direct the kids to begin.

This is for you, Ellie Sander, who makes all things possible. Who makes kids laugh and grown-ups smile and flowers bloom—in the darnedest places. Who put Humpty Dumpty back together again...and made Georgie Porgy consider not running away.

Damn.

Mitch almost missed a beat.

Ellie made all things possible. Even falling in love.

The broad expanses of KirkKnoll Park swarmed with people leaving the concert. Ellie rolled King's wheelchair to the edge of the sidewalk, out of the paths of passersby. Where were her children? Where was Mitch? Should she set the brake and wait a little longer, or should they just go home?

"Maybe they're having an after-show party." She managed to sound almost cheerful in spite of her growing worry.

Harriet straightened King's collar and smiled down at him. "They'll be along, won't they, King?"

He patted her hand. "I'd bet my flügelhorn on it."

Ellie's heart gave a little twist of envy. She hadn't noticed before the feelings that seemed to be growing between King and Harriet. Mitch had actually shown some feelings for his father tonight, too. She should be happy her plan had accomplished at least that.

"Mom!"

Through the throng of people she caught sight of Michael zigzagging like a football player, followed by his two brothers. But where was—?

"Mommy, look at me!"

The crowd parted, and Mitch strode through, with Seri perched high on his shoulders.

Ellie couldn't tell which of them grinned the widest. On second glance, she realized Mitch was smiling through gritted teeth. Seri held a death grip on his hair.

"Seri, honey, you're hurt—"

Mitch shook his head, then winced. "It's all right."

"Seri!" King boomed. "Come down here. I have to ask you and your brothers something."

Curiosity overrode Seri's reluctance to give up her high perch. Carefully Mitch lifted her to the ground. She dashed over to King.

"When we stop at the ice-cream shop," he asked, "do you want Marshmallow-Pretzel-Butterfly-Chunk or Peanut-Banana-Ladybug-Chip?"

King's good spirits filled Ellie with gratitude. She was so glad they'd managed to bring him here tonight. So very happy about Mitch's introduction.

A space cleared on the sidewalk, and she maneuvered King's wheelchair forward, keeping an eye out for her kids. But she needn't have worried. They stayed glued to King's side, caught up in outdoing his outrageous ice-cream flavors.

King's charm seemed to know few boundaries, Ellie mused. He was making even tough-minded Harriet Givens giggle. If only Ellie could pretend Mitch was part of this strange mixture of extended family. Just for this evening.

She allowed herself a quick glance where he ambled beside her. He returned her gaze, the corners of his mouth tugging upward, the lines around his eyes crinkling softly.

All her hopes rose from the ashes of last evening.

"Here, let me push." He reached to take the wheelchair handles, sliding his hands over the tops of hers.

His touch sent waves of pleasure floating through her. Reluctantly, she slid her hands away, but he caught her by the wrist, tucked her hand through his arm and held it in place long enough to let her know he wanted her to keep it there. The gesture dissolved all her caution.

Under her fingertips, his light gray jacket felt smooth and crisp. His brisk, pine scent made her light-headed and muzzy. In another second she would probably just melt altogether.

She stifled a giggle. Mitch would have to carry her. The idea had definite appeal.

He glanced down at her quizzically. "You really put one over on me tonight. How the devil did you get King here?"

She cocked her head. "A little Yankee ingenuity. And a whole lot of luck. I owed you this one, Mitch, after the help you gave me with my parents. Besides, I wanted King to enjoy the results of your work together."

King twisted around in his wheelchair. "King Kole's Kids have never sung better," he bellowed. "I was proud to be there," he added more seriously. "You did a great job, son."

Ellie held her breath. She'd planned the whole evening for the one kind of happy ending she'd let her foolish heart seek. Mitch's words from the stage had brought tears to her eyes, but this was up close and personal—just between Mitch and King.

She felt the muscles of his arm tighten, read the conflict in his eyes. Sensed his urge to cut and run.

He reached up to touch her hand, all the while searching her face. As if he were seeking courage.

"Actually I ended up kind of enjoying the little critters," he admitted, but his grin diminished in spite of the kids' loud protests. He looked away from Ellie. Turned to face King. "I'm glad you were there, Dad. I'm glad I came home."

Ellie's heart soared. She wanted to hug Mitch. She wanted to kiss him. She wanted—

"Here, Ellie." From his pocket, he pulled a small tape recorder. "This is for you."

"A recording of this evening," King added. "Mitch and I thought you might like to have it."

Hesitantly she reached for the little black instrument. Could something so small really capture all of this magical evening: Mitch's warm introduction, King's hearty laughter, her children's sweet voices? The happy humming of her own heart? Could this little device really hold all the sounds of a family, the laughter, the closeness. The love?

Tonight—for a few shining moments—she felt it might still be possible to have a whole family. A family filled with love.

A fairy-tale family…with this man.

In spite of all her father's warnings, this was what she still dared to wish for.

Chapter Nine

"**W**e *did* it!" Rafe shouted.

"Yes!" Michael shot a fist in the air.

Mitch settled King into his wheelchair and rolled him into the main room, then returned to stare back down the cardboard-lined staircase. *Unbelievable!* Ellie and her kids had built King an escape chute, a way out of the castle he'd been imprisoned in for almost a month.

Ellie was even more amazing than he'd imagined.

From the landing, he watched her moving around the room, turning on lamps that cast a warm glow on her family. Bubba Sue pranced beside the chair as Gabe wheeled King to the TV. Harriet produced a thermometer and handed it to Seri who popped it into King's mouth while Harriet checked his pulse.

What a scene. Hearth and home. Norman Rockwell a la nineties.

Mitch lay aside the straps and clips he'd just removed from King and forced his attention to coiling the rope. A routine procedure, one he'd done maybe a hundred times. Which was good, because he couldn't seem to stay focused.

Except on Ellie. The way her blue sundress brushed her legs as she moved. The way her hair glinted with threads of gold. The memory of her hand resting on his arm all the way back to the flat—as if she belonged there beside him.

Ellie watched out for her kids like a cat with a litter of mischievous kittens. She cared for King like a clucking mother hen and welcomed Harriet as if she were a wise grandmother owl. Ellie accepted *him,* mule-headed as he was, as if he were someone special. As if he were part of this ragtag accumulation of people she cared about. Part of her family.

All evening he'd felt it—the warmth, the belonging, the sense of family. It went against everything he'd ever allowed himself to think about. It felt better than anything he'd ever dreamed. It terrified him.

His father had failed the greatest responsibilities of having a family. Mitch could never risk doing the same.

"How are you feeling, King?"

Ellie's gentle concern tumbled what little self-defense Mitch had managed to start rebuilding.

"I'm feeling just *fine,*" King bellowed. "I've got broken *bones,* not the chicken pox, for crying out loud."

Ellie planted a slender finger in the middle of King's chest. "You've had an exhausting day. It's time for you to be in *bed.*"

Her sassy, presumptuous care made Mitch quake with envy.

"You, too!" She pointed to her children.

What about *him?* Ellie threatened everything about life as he knew it, but, heaven help him, he didn't want this to end.

"Aw, Mom, can't we watch TV?"

Mitch strode into the room, near enough to catch Ellie's sweet, fresh scent, to see her pupils widen. "Half an hour won't hurt them, Ellie."

"But King was already up late last—"

"I think King's just fine." Harriet smiled mischievously. "Would you like me to stay a bit longer—just to make sure?"

Last chance to change his mind, to send everyone scattering, to break this illusion that he was part of a big happy family. But he wanted time with Ellie alone.

Ellie moved to the wheelchair. "No, thanks, Harriet—"

"*Yes,* thanks." Mitch overrode her. Taking her hand, he pulled her toward the kitchen. "I want to show you something."

"But, Mitch—"

"Shhh. No protests."

She followed him, slowly at first, holding back, full of hesitation. Her hand felt small and soft in his, and he held it more tightly, unsure which of them was shaking.

The kitchen was filled with shadows save for the flicker of the television from the next room. Ellie reached for the light switch. "It's awfully dark in here."

But he held her fast, tugged her firmly into his arms.

"Mitch?" Her voice trembled. Even in the shadows, her eyes were big and full of uncertainty. He wanted to hold her, to protect her, to let her know she was safe with him. But how could he tell her something so untrue? She wasn't safe, would never be safe with a man who couldn't take on the full-time responsibilities of another person's well-being. Of other people's *lives.*

He watched her uncurl her fingers and slowly rest her

hands on his chest. A gesture of trust. But he was so unworthy.

"Mitch," she murmured. "I think—"

"Don't think," he whispered. Unable to stop himself, he dipped his head to brush her cheek, to feel the silk of her hair against his face. God, she was sweet, sweeter than anything he'd ever known. Drifting to the hollow beneath her ear, he caught her lobe between his lips, tasted the honey of her skin. Heard her catch her breath.

She slid her hands around his neck, drew herself tightly against him, making him groan at the soft fullness of her breasts. At his growing hardness. Her breathing became shallow. Matching his own.

Don't think, he warned himself. Because he didn't want this heat to cool; he didn't want this to stop. Even if he did something foolhardy, like telling her how much he wanted her.

Like telling her he loved her.

He loved her. The realization rocked him again. What he felt for Ellie went way beyond wanting. Panicked, he pulled back to look down at her. What he saw in her face destroyed any resistance he might have hoped to salvage.

Her eyes were dark, yearning, smoky with desire. But there was something more. Not the wariness and resentment he'd seen in her that first morning. Something he'd never seen in a woman's eyes before. Except in his mother's.

Sadness. The sight made his chest ache.

"Mom?"

Come on, Gabe. Not now.

Slowly Ellie pulled away from him, breaking the contact of their bodies, stealing her lush, desirous warmth.

But she didn't stop watching him with those sad, questioning eyes.

"What is it, sweetheart?"

"There's a message on the answering machine." Gabe sounded very young...and scared.

"It's for Mitch. Some guy named Jack." Gabe's voice grew tougher as he spoke. "Sounds like an *emergency*." Sarcasm dripped from the last of his words as he whirled from the kitchen doorway.

Jack. Mitch's friend and mentor. Jack, who had been like a substitute father to him. Jack and Josey were the only family Mitch allowed himself. No strings attached.

Somehow Ellie knew that.

He watched her sadness deepen, because she understood, just as his mother had. Kole men always went away.

Ellie tried not to listen, but she couldn't help herself. *"Mitch, it's Jack. Sorry I missed your call last night. We were tracking a lost hiker. Still missing. We could sure use your help. By the way, your B and B renovation is still stalled and there's an east-coast conglomerate making take-over noises about Winterhaven. Hope your dad's doing better. Josey can meet you at the airport if you come. Gotta run."* The message ended with a beep.

Turning on the faucet, she let the blast of water drown out the silence that followed. She held her hands under the cold water, then splashed it onto her face, washing away the trace of a tear that had slipped down her cheek, failing to wash away the memory of Mitch's kisses.

She'd let herself forget. The whole time Mitch had been here, the clock had been ticking. She just hadn't expected him to be called away by the beep of an answering machine.

Cinderella of the nineties, she thought sorrowfully. How had she allowed herself to care so much? When would she learn there was no such thing as a happy ending?

She turned the faucet off and reached for a towel. Behind her, footsteps scuffed the tile floor.

"Ellie, I... It was my friend Jack. From Colorado." Mitch sounded almost apologetic.

She didn't turn around. Those dark blue eyes, full of the urgency to flee, would be more than she could stand. "I'm...sure you're glad to hear from him."

"Yeah, well... He's sort of like...an uncle or something. Gave me a job. Taught me how to ski..." Mitch sounded as if there was much more he wanted to say.

Tears threatened again. Ellie stared out the window, but all she could see in the bright light was her reflection staring sadly back. Blinking hard, she looked down. "He must be...important to you."

"He is."

She heard him move around the counter, could almost feel his body heat and the disquiet that seemed to emanate from him.

"Ellie, there's a lost hiker. Jack *never* asks for help, but...he wouldn't have called if he didn't need it." He hesitated. "I can get a flight tonight. I should be back in time for King's doctor appointment."

Why did his statements sound more like questions? He was going and they both knew it. She'd been expecting it; she'd known all along The Prince wasn't a family man. She'd been prepared for this, hadn't she?

Swallowing back tears, she turned to face him. "It's all right, Mitch. After tonight, you shouldn't have any doubts about how well we can manage. Your father is much better, and Harriet... I think she'll be available whenever we need her. You don't need to worry about coming back.''

Mitch moved nearer. ''Ellie, I won't leave you to—''

''No, really, Mitch, it's okay.'' She tried to clear the knot from her throat. ''You've done your duty…and more.'' With her back to the counter, she slipped along its length, keeping her distance from him. ''You made your father very happy tonight.'' The words caught in her throat.

Skirting him, she reached the doorway to the main room. She needed her kids. More than anything, right now she needed to be near them, to feel their trust, their love.

''You're still free, you know.'' She forced the words around the ache. ''You can go back to your exciting life any time you choose. We don't need you here anymore.''

She stepped into the room, and her heart fell another mile. King sat beside Harriet with Bubba Sue in his lap. Her kids lay at their feet entwined like a mess of fishing worms. Except for the fact that Rafe had the phone again, and Michael rattled an ongoing interpretation of the show, no one seemed particularly upset. They were a tight-knit unit huddled around King and Harriet. They acted as if she weren't even there.

Even Seri.

''Seri?'' She scanned the tangle of kids for Seri's flyaway topknot in the pink scrunchy. It wasn't sticking up above the heads of her curly-topped brothers.

Seri wasn't there.

Crossing the room, Ellie hurried down the hall to the master bedroom, swiping away the tears that broke through her lashes. Darn it, she would *not* cry. She'd known she shouldn't fall in love with Mitch. Her heart just hadn't been paying attention.

But neither had Seri. Seri hadn't even *tried* not to love him. She'd come to care about him as much as Ellie had, which was why she had to show her daughter how to say goodbye.

"Seri?" She rushed into the bedroom. The night-light cast a muted aqua glow, filling the corners with shadows. Any one of them could be her sad little daughter.

"Seri, honey?" Ellie snapped on the light. The room was empty.

"Se-ri?" She turned back into the hall, checked the bathroom. The walk-in closet.

No sign of her daughter.

A sharp point of fear pierced her concern.

She mustn't overreact. Seri was in the Mermaid Room. Somehow she'd managed to slip past Mitch and her in the kitchen. Probably looking for her stuffed animals. For hugs and reassurance. The same things Ellie needed now—terribly.

She retraced her steps through the living room, barely glancing at the group in front of the TV except to note that Mitch hadn't joined them.

He was probably packing already. She didn't think her heart could drop any lower. But it did.

She strode down the hall, whirled into the Mermaid Room and flicked on the light. "Seri?"

Seri's teddy bear and tiger lay on the bed.

Now she was running, across the hall to the big bathroom. Empty. On to the dormitory where Mitch leaned over a bed folding things into a backpack.

"Have you seen Seri? Is she here with you?" She hated that she sounded so frightened. So out of control.

Mitch turned to search her face. "Ellie, what's the

matter? I haven't seen her since—'' he hesitated
"—since the phone message." He sounded suddenly
contrite. "I remember seeing her climb from Harriet's
lap and head toward the kitchen. I thought she was looking for you."

But Ellie had *been* in the kitchen. Why hadn't she
seen her daughter? Because she'd been crying over another unhappy ending, crying over another highway
man. She hadn't been there when her daughter needed
her.

She spun away, only half aware of Mitch's footsteps
behind her down the hall. In the main room, she rushed
over to flip the TV off. "Everybody up and search this
house until you find your sister," she commanded.
"Now!"

She must have looked as scared as she felt because
her sons scattered without protests—followed by the little black dog. Harriet and Mitch went, too. Lights flashed
on, doors opened, the flat rang with shouts, but when
everyone regrouped around a scowling King, they shook
their heads silently.

"The store," King exclaimed. "She told me she liked
to sit in the storage room when she was missing her
daddy," he added quietly. "Maybe she slipped down the
back stairs."

Heart hammering, Ellie ran through the kitchen and
down the stairs, footsteps pounding behind her. *Oh,
please, dear God, let Seri be in the store.*

At the bottom, she grabbed the doorknob and shoved.
The door didn't budge. It was locked! Ellie's heart all
but stopped. Seri couldn't be in the store.

Where could she be?

"Mom! Look!"

She turned to where Gabe pointed, to the door leading

outside, the door that should have been closed tight and guarded with a security alarm.

The door stood ajar.

"Now don't you worry, Mrs. Sander. You just sit tight, and we'll call you first thing when we find your daughter." Police Officer Linley gathered his hat and notes and stood up.

If it hadn't been for Mitch standing beside her, Ellie might have been intimidated by the six-foot-six officer, even though he looked as if he'd just graduated from high school. So help her, though, if he patted her on the head, she wouldn't be responsible for what she said.

"Please, Officer Linley...just go look for her."

"Right." He headed down the front stairs. "I'll let myself out. Now, you just call the KPD if you think of anything else."

Ellie waited till she heard the click of the latch below. *"KPD?"* She turned to Mitch. "I'm supposed to rely on a rookie cop who's seen too much TV? I'm supposed to stay calm while my *daughter* is missing?"

"Now, Ellie, he's doing his job."

Mitch was trying to soothe her. She didn't want to be soothed.

"I'm not supposed to *worry?* What does a kid like that know about having a four-year-old daughter wandering the streets late at night? *Alone!"* Ellie perched on the edge of the sofa and hugged Seri's jacket close, trying to hold off panic.

"I'm supposed to sit *tight?"* She jolted back up and began pacing. "How can I sit at all when those kids on roller skates might be chasing her?" *Or some pervert trying to lure her into his car?*

She inhaled sharply. The scene she'd been trying not to imagine sent a shaft of terror knifing through her.

"Ellie, don't—"

"I can't help it, Mitch." Anguish tightened her chest. "I *can't* sit waiting while my baby's in danger." A surge of adrenaline shot through her. "I *won't*." She marched into the kitchen, yanked open a drawer and searched for a flashlight. Behind her she heard a muffled oath.

"What are you *doing?*"

"I'm going to look for my daughter."

"Then I'm going with you."

"I thought you were leaving."

This time he swore vividly. "Look, this is my old neighborhood, Ellie. I used to roam it at night. I know where kids hide. I won't let you go alone."

She rounded on him with anguish that burst into fury. "You won't *let* me?"

He actually winced; there was some gratification in that, though none in the misery she found in his eyes.

"Ellie, I didn't mean—"

He didn't mean to sound as if he cared about *her,* that was what he really meant. Right now, that made her furious. Pushed her to the edge.

"We were doing just fine before you got here, Mitch. I told you before—we don't need your help. The boys don't need a role model and Seri doesn't need a Prince Charming and King has Harriet now, so he doesn't need you, either." Dragging in a painful breath, she looked over the brink, then stepped off.

"Seri is *my* responsibility, Mitch, not yours. I don't *want* you here anymore."

Pain slashed across his face, and she knew she'd struck home. But there was no satisfaction in it.

He took a step forward, as if to reach for her. Then he stopped. "I'm not leaving until we find Seri."

She should send him away right now. She shouldn't let him come to their rescue. But she needed his help. Seri needed it. She'd have to deal with her feelings later.

"All right. I'll get a sweater." She found one on the back of a chair and folded Seri's jacket into the pocket. In the main room she checked that her sons hadn't gone off on a search of their own. She couldn't bear having another child unaccounted for. To her relief, they were all still there, sticking close to Harriet and King.

"Boys, I want you in bed. Harriet, can you stay and help King?"

"Don't worry, Ellie. I'll take care of things here. You and Mitch just go find our little princess."

She and Mitch. The words stirred a flicker of hope. But it quickly flared into anger. Mitch didn't care about Seri. He was going with Ellie because that was what he did—search for lost people. As soon as he finished here, he'd still leave, to go search for that lost hiker in the mountains. It seemed to be the only kind of responsibility he took on. Of short duration. Impersonal.

She had to stop nursing foolish dreams.

"Let's go, Mitch." Shaking herself, she plunged down the stairs to the door.

The street outside loomed dark and uninviting. Shadows hovered along the buildings like prowling demons, and trees rustled as if dark creatures lurked in their branches. A sharp crack made her gasp, sent her heartbeat skyrocketing. She clutched her sweater closer.

Mitch switched on the flashlight. "It was just a tree branch, Ellie."

"I know. But if I'm jumping at creaking branches, Seri must be terrified. We've got to find her."

"We will. Come on." He set off down the sidewalk. "I think we should go to the park. It's her favorite place."

"But it's such an enormous place..." Full of too many nooks and hollows where a little girl could hide. Where she could fall into an exhausted sleep and not hear her mother's voice. It would take them a long time to search the whole park.

Mitch strode beside her. "I think I have an idea where she might be."

"You *know* where she is?" She stared up at him. "Why didn't you *say* so? Where *is* she?"

"I didn't think of it before, but there's this place in the park..."

Ellie started to run. "Show me!"

Mitch caught up with her. "There's a bunch of bushes near the amphitheater. They make a little alcove. I showed it to her on the way to practice one day. I...told her it was Sleeping Beauty's castle," he added quietly.

They entered the park, and he led her onto one of the serpentine paths. The trees cast mottled shadows, and strange, dark shapes loomed everywhere. In the dark, the park became an evil, bewitched forest. Just like in Sleeping Beauty, Ellie thought. She fought an urge to reach for Mitch's hand.

"Are you sure this is the right way?"

"Yes. Here, take the flashlight. I know the park at night."

There was a reason for that, one she'd probably never know. Right now nothing mattered except finding her baby.

Beyond a rise, the curve of the amphitheater shell appeared. Mitch jogged ahead, then slowed. He scanned the area, then cut across the lawn toward a dark dome of bushes.

Ellie shined the light ahead. Started to run. "Seri? *Seri,* where are you?"

"Mommy?" A small, scared voice called from the tangle of branches.

In an instant, Ellie was at their edge and on her knees crawling, clambering in, sliding the light ahead of her.

"Seri, honey, where are you, baby? Mommy's coming."

"Mommy, Mommy…"

With Seri's every sob, Ellie's heart broke a little more. She pushed through the branches, yanking her sweater loose, ignoring the dirt and twigs digging into her knees.

"It's okay, baby, Mommy's here." Then she was scooping Seri into her arms, holding her, rocking her, crooning soothing sounds through her own tears. "It's okay, baby."

Mitch's face appeared in a shadowy opening. "Is she all right?"

Seri stiffened in Ellie's arms.

Using the pale beam of the flashlight, Ellie checked her daughter more carefully. No bruises, no blood, nothing torn. Dirt streaked her white blouse and there were leaves in her flyaway hair. Her pink hair scrunchy was gone, but the big pink rabbit lay nearby.

"Are you okay, sweetheart? Did Rabbit take care of you?"

Seri nodded, though tears still tracked her cheeks and her bottom lip quivered.

"Hey, Princess, I see you're awake."

In spite of everything, the gentleness of Mitch's voice touched Ellie. But Seri clung to her, burying her face in her shoulder.

"Take me home, Mommy."

"Here, Ellie, let me carry her." Mitch reached for her.

"*Noooo,*" Seri wailed, shrinking away.

"Seri, honey, what is it?"

Seri held Ellie's neck tighter. "I thought he was going to be my daddy. But he's going away, *too,* isn't he?"

"Oh, Seri." The very thing she'd tried so hard to protect her daughter from. Ellie looked regretfully at Mitch. If only he could help her *now*. But she could find only anguish in his face.

Seri put her hands on Ellie's cheeks. "Mommy?"

"What, precious?" Tears of love and sympathy brimmed Ellie's eyes.

"Please take me home. I don't want to be Sleeping Beauty. I don't believe in princes anymore."

Chapter Ten

Mitch held the front door of the flat for Ellie, trying hard not to look at the wispy-haired child clinging to her shoulder. No longer the little Princess who had presented herself so regally that first morning he'd awakened in a sea of mermaids. Gone the sprightly curiosity, the bold expectations, the serious, big brown eyes. Seri had become a frightened, disillusioned little...realist.

All because of him.

But at least she was alive. At least no harm had come to her because of his bad judgment.

No harm had come to her mother. Yet.

Sweet, courageous Ellie. He couldn't stop watching her as she climbed the stairs ahead of him, her white sandals bruised with dirt, the hem of her once-crisp sundress soiled and uneven, her saggy brown sweater snagged with twigs. But despite the leaves still clinging to her dusty blond hair, it swung soft and silky around her shoulders, and she carried her daughter with a back stiff with determination. Without looking, he already knew the angle of her chin.

Proud woman. Strong-headed. Strong-hearted. Far too good for the likes of him, even if he was in love with her. But loving wasn't enough—his father had already proven that.

It was time to leave. As soon as he saw to it that everyone was okay, he'd grab a cab to a motel and catch the first plane out in the morning.

Mitch shifted the big pink rabbit Seri had finally agreed to let him carry and glanced through the stair rail. The flat seemed uncharacteristically quiet.

"I'll check on King while you get Seri into bed," he whispered.

"I bet Harriet already has him—"

The rumble of running feet overrode her words.

"*Mom!* Hey, *they're back!* Is she okay?"

"Where was she?"

"Did you get to ride in a police car?"

Mitch tried to step aside, but the three boys and one excited dog circled Ellie like moons jostling their way into safe orbits again. Somehow Mitch got swept along, through the dimly lit rooms and down the hall until they burst into the dormitory.

"Look, they're back!" Michael shouted.

In a glance, Mitch took in the scene. King sat in bed propped against a wall of pillows, buried under a mound of paper flowers. He was grinning. Harriet rushed forward, arms open to engulf them in a hug. Neither King nor Harriet bothered to hide their tears. Bubba Sue jumped onto Mitch's bed and settled in next to his half-packed backpack.

Mitch's agitation gave way to regret.

"Look, Seri, we made you flowers." Gabe picked a pink one and held it out to her.

Harriet lifted Seri from Ellie's arms and kissed her cheek. "Come here, sweetheart." Sitting her on the bed beside King, she handed her another flower.

"Welcome home, Princess." King wrapped her in a grandfatherly hug, then laid more flowers in her lap.

Those flowers again. Always showing up when someone wanted to show care or concern. And here was his father, giving them out like the presents he used to bring his mother. Presents and paper flowers. Maybe the message was the same.

Seri laid King's flowers with the others on the bed. "Thank you. But I'm not going to be a princess anymore."

Mitch watched with growing turmoil as King tucked a wisp of hair behind Seri's ear.

"How come, little one?"

Slowly she turned to look at Mitch.

Déjà vu.

He'd never known one little girl's grave brown eyes could inflict so much pain.

"*Are* you going away?"

He'd asked his father the same question at least a thousand times. With always the same answer.

"Seri, I—" He watched her eyes brim with tears. Felt ambivalence slice through him. She wasn't asking about a short trip. She was asking about forever.

He'd let things go too far. He'd soaked up the warm fuzzies of Ellie's family like some dried old sponge. He'd encouraged make-believe that had put Seri in real danger. He'd put his own needs ahead of theirs.

He couldn't give them what they needed. He couldn't

risk it, because he was too damn much like his father. Couldn't live up to commitments.

"Yes, Seri. I'm going."

Seri's lip quivered, but she held his gaze. Her little chin tilted up. Just like her mother.

Mitch felt his throat tighten. Damned if he hadn't come to love this little imp. Unwillingly, his gaze shifted to the three boys leaning against Ellie. Rebellious Gabe, compulsive Michael, needy Rafe with a viselike grip on her skirt—all of them staring up at him with condemnation. The worst of it was that he cared—he cared how they felt! He didn't want to hurt them anymore. Which probably meant he loved the boys, too.

No. He couldn't let that happen.

"I'll wait till you're all settled. Then I'll catch a cab."

The boys seemed to shrink tighter against Ellie. Scooping Seri onto her hip, she chose a flower from among those on the bed and moved toward him with all her children in tow.

"We want to say goodbye, don't we, kids? And to thank you for the help...with your father." Her voice wavered. In spite of the shadows under her eyes, color tinged her cheeks. But her back remained broomstick straight.

"Kids, say goodbye to Mitch."

Seri buried her head in Ellie's shoulder, but Ellie nudged her up. "Come on, baby. Boys?"

Painful silence yielded to a barely audible, "Bye." An unwilling group grunt. He didn't blame them. All they knew was that he was just another man walking out on them. The thought caused a physical ache in his chest.

"Bye, gang." The words came hard. He searched for

something to soften the bluntness, but what more could he say without increasing the damage?

"Okay, enough of goodbyes." Harriet lifted Seri from Ellie's arms. "It's time for toothbrushes and PJ's. Everybody get ready for bed." She moved toward the big bathroom, hustling the boys before her.

Mitch dragged his gaze from Ellie's. "I'll get King settled." He stepped aside to let her leave.

"Before I tuck them in, I need to talk to you." She led him down the hallway, away from his father, away from Harriet and the kids and the rush of running water.

Inside the kitchen, she switched on the light. Straightened a drawing on the refrigerator door. Stared at the paper flower in her hand. Finally she looked up.

"Mitch...?" Her eyes no longer snapped with arctic cold but clouded with a misty blue sadness. "Thanks for what you did for your dad. For your help with my kids. With Seri."

Her words tightened the ache in his chest. "Ellie, you're the one who deserves—"

"I might not have found Seri without you."

The light in the room glared harsh and accusing. "Without me, she never would have been lost," he blurted bitterly.

He had to fight a need to reach out and brush a smudge of dirt from her cheek. Even now, he couldn't help thinking—just two steps and the top of her head would barely brush his chin. But he shouldn't even be here.

"I need to go help King. And finish packing."

She held out her hand. "This is for you."

The flower? She was offering it to *him?*

"Ellie...I don't need your—"

"I want you to have it, Mitch. Just to sort of say...remember us."

As if he needed anything to make him remember. Only Ellie would give a gift to a man who was running away again. But he didn't have it in him to refuse. Taking care not to touch her, he reached for the flower.

"Goodbye, Mitch," she whispered. Then she fled.

He stood there listening to the chatter rise as she found her children and herded them into the Mermaid Room. Suddenly he wanted to tear the damn flower into a million pieces. He wanted to hurl it through a window like a rock. If only he had the courage to go after her. Take her into his arms. Never let her go.

But he didn't.

Stuffing the flower into his shirt pocket, he strode back to the dormitory.

King lay against the mound of pillows, his eyes closed. At the sound of Mitch's footsteps, he looked up.

"I was hoping you'd come back, son."

Son. He didn't want to hear it. He and his father had smoothed a lot of ground, but he didn't want to be reminded of the loss that still lay between them. He straightened the covers, then reached for the switch to lower the bed. "I'll try to get back in time to help Ellie take you to the doctor."

"She loves you, you know."

Mitch straightened abruptly. All the frustration and fear of the last few hours came boiling to the surface. "What do *you* know about loving?"

Anguish flickered across King's face.

Suddenly Mitch wanted to call the words back. "Dad, I'm...sorry."

"I know, son. I am, too. I should have told you long ago, I would give my life to have been here that night.

I shouldn't have traveled so much. I should have been here—for both of you.'' He paled noticeably, seemed to struggle for air.

Fear knifed through Mitch's confusion. He moved forward, but his father held up a hand.

''I made terrible mistakes, Mitch.'' His voice grew gravelly with emotion. ''But *you* can learn from them. Come back home…or take Ellie and her kids with you. Be together. Love each other. That's all that matters.''

''Ellie doesn't love me.'' And he would get over loving her. It was safer not to love at all.

''I happen to know that flower sticking out of your pocket isn't a KirkKnoll souvenir, son. Ellie loves you, all right. That's what the flowers mean.''

Ellie tipped the coffeepot to pour half the water down the sink, then emptied the rest into the opening of the brewer. No need to make a full pot anymore. Grabbing the fourth cup on the counter, she shoved it back into the cupboard.

Her reflection stared back at her from the glass doors of the cabinet, dark circles under red-rimmed eyes. Evidence of the terrible emptiness she felt inside.

Mitch was gone. She'd heard him go. She'd lain awake last night listening for the muffled click of the door latch and the acceleration of the taxi. She'd stayed awake longer, rocked by her daughter's silent sobs. Fighting tears of her own. She hadn't known how quickly Mitch could become part of their lives. She thought she'd guarded against him stealing into their hearts.

Shaking herself, she pulled up straighter. She had to show her kids a better example than this. She tugged cereal out of the cupboard and set it on the counter. No pancakes today. They didn't need reminders of that first morning. Just juice and sugar critters and get the boys off to their last week of school.

Then she'd make a work schedule.

Work was the solution to every problem—that was what her father always preached. She'd keep her kids so busy, like Seri's big pink rabbit, just going...and going...until they forgot about Mitch.

Reaching into the refrigerator, she set out juice and milk. Who needed Mitch, anyway? With King growing stronger every day and Harriet coming extra time, they'd manage fine. They had King's routine down perfectly.

They'd been doing just fine before Mitch showed up in the first place. She slapped bowls down on the counter. He needn't have bothered coming, sneaking in that first night, falling asleep in the middle of Seri's mermaids...like an unexpected sea god.

She glanced again at her reflection, half expecting to see her nose starting to grow. Ashamed of the tears gathering in her eyes. Because she was lying. Because the truth hurt so much.

They might not *need* Mitch's help anymore, but she wanted him here. Her *kids* wanted him here. She'd fallen in love with him, so how could she expect her kids to be immune? She could even understand Seri running away. Discovering Prince Charming might not want to stay around was a pretty harsh lesson for a four-year-old.

But she couldn't blame Mitch, either. No man—prince *nor* commoner—wanted a frazzled homeless mother of four kids. A woman definitely not of a sweet and docile nature. Couldn't waltz till midnight if her life depended on it. Usually asleep on her feet before nine-thirty.

And fairy godmothers were impossible to come by nowadays.

But Mitch had said he'd come back. He'd left her with hope. She was counting on the power in that one small paper blossom.

Foolish woman. Incurable dreamer. She was bound to wind up with a broken heart.

But she'd never let her kids know.

Ellie swished water around in the tub, swirling the scouring powder down the drain. Pushing to her feet, she dropped the soiled towels into the hamper and headed for the kitchen. The tape recorder in her sweater pocket slapped against her thigh.

Why did she torture herself?

From the other end of the flat, laughter and barking bubbled out of the dormitory. The first signs of rising spirits she'd heard all week. Thank goodness.

The boys must be home from school. Time to give them their assignments for the day. She snatched up the job list from the counter and marched down the hall. As she drew nearer, the chatter in the dormitory faltered, then stopped abruptly, followed by a cacophony of squeaking bedsprings.

"Hey, Mom."

She entered the room just as Rafe wiggled in between Seri and Michael on the nearest of the beds. On the next bed, Gabe adjusted a pile of pillows behind his head and Bubba Sue settled in next to him. Between the two beds, King maneuvered his wheelchair as if he were practicing parallel parking.

Ellie's mother sensors sounded Alert. Everyone looked guilty as sin. Even the dog!

"What are you up to?"

"Nothing." Gabe sounded more innocent than he'd managed since he was seven.

Ellie eyed them suspiciously. Something *was* going on. They'd been grumpy and whiny all week, but now they seemed...different. Almost energized.

Out of the corner of her eye, she saw Michael stuff something into his pocket. "What have you been doing?"

Michael jerked Seri's shirttail, then nodded guiltily and pulled a cookie from his pocket.

"Michael, you know I don't want crumbs all over in here. Your first job will be to shake off the beds and sweep the floor. Gabe, I want you to scrub the shower walls. Rafe, you and Seri fold the clean laundry on the sofa. When you finish, check with me."

"Aww, *Mo*-om!" Michael bounced onto his stomach and glared up at her.

"We've been working *every day*," Gabe groused.

"I don't *want* to work any more," Rafe added.

"Me, *neither!*" Seri rolled over beside Michael and stuck out her bottom lip.

Her daughter looked so indignant, Ellie almost laughed. This was more like it. They were getting their energy back. A good sign the storm was lifting, the memories of Mitch fading.

She touched the black box in her sweater pocket and wished she could say the same for herself.

King rolled his chair nearer. "Sounds like mutiny to me. Ellie, why don't you tear up that list and take these scallywags to the park. It's a beautiful day, too good to waste on work."

Because tomorrow is Friday, that's why. The day King was to go back to the doctor. Mitch had said he would try to return to help, but they hadn't heard one word from him. She didn't want them to remember.

"There'll be plenty of park days after school is out, but spring cleaning should be done in the spring. Let's go, gang."

This time the bedsprings groaned as her children dragged themselves up, muttering and complaining. Even the dog whined.

King wheeled himself after them. "Michael, before you sweep in here, please go down to the store and ask Robin to count the supply of reeds. And stay till she gives you the answer."

Ellie studied King while she waited for her kids to file out. Her mother sensors still flashed Alert. King was making work for Michael so he'd leave along with the others. Something fishy *was* going on.

"Ellie…?" King wheeled around to face her. "Do you know where that recording is…from the other night?"

"Omigod." Hastily she dug the tape recorder from her pocket and handed it to him. "I'm sorry, King." Heat crept up her neck. She'd been mooning around all week listening to Mitch's voice without a thought for King's feelings. He might like to listen to the concert, too.

"Ellie, I need to tell you something."

Sheepishly she settled on the edge of the bed. She'd been so intent on forgetting Mitch, she'd overlooked that his father might be hurting, too.

"What is it, King?"

He wheeled his chair nearer. "I never told you about my wife…Jeanne. You remind me of her." He smiled. "She was the most patient, most understanding wife a man could ever have."

Why was King telling her this?

"We had a son, a kid full of sass and vinegar." His voice took on more of the bluster she was used to. So it was Mitch he wanted to talk about, after all.

"He was talented, too. I hoped he'd grow up to make music with my little group, King Kole and his Merry Men. Sounds kind of corny now, but back then we made pretty good jazz. Traveled a lot. I thought if we got known, we might make it to the big time."

He hesitated, then fiddled with the tape recorder. "That was my dream—for my wife and my kid. At least, that's what I told myself. So I went off to make music. Left them a lot."

She could see him struggle. "King, you don't have to—"

He raised a hand. "I want you to know, Ellie. When Mitch was about fourteen, his mother got sick…late one night while I was on the road. Mitch wanted to call an ambulance, but she wouldn't let him. She was like that, never complaining, always expecting the best of things. When she finally became unconscious, he called for help."

Ellie's hand flew to her heart.

"By then it was too late."

"Oh, King, no…"

"She'd insisted it was just a bad case of stomach flu. Turned out, it was a ruptured aneurysm. She died on the way to the hospital."

"King, I'm so sorry…" For King. For the terrified boy Mitch must have been.

"At first Mitch blamed me for not being there. Later, I believe he started to blame himself."

"Oh." Now she understood the terrible tension between Mitch and his father. Now she understood a lot of things about Mitch. "But it wasn't his fault. It wasn't anybody's—"

"If I'd been here, I might have gotten her to the hospital sooner."

King's anguish hung in the air. Ellie didn't know how to answer, so she reached for his hand.

He held on to her tightly. "Mitch was just a kid, Ellie. He was so shattered. He wouldn't go with me to counseling, wouldn't even talk to me. Just pulled into himself. Stayed out late. Got into trouble. Finally he ran away. He wasn't quite seventeen."

"Oh, King..." She remembered Mitch's allusions to late night roaming in KirkKnoll.

"I'd about given up finding him when Jack Winter called from Colorado. He and his wife had taken him in, sent him back to school, given him a job. Mitch refused to come home." His voice broke.

Ellie held his hands while he struggled to regain control.

At last, he pulled himself up in the chair. "Ellie, I lost a wife *and* a son. I gave up all those years we could have been together *before* she died. I threw away the present for a future that never came."

He enclosed her hand in both of his. "Don't do the same with the people you love, Ellie. Let them know you love them."

Ellie blinked back tears. "You're right." What was one little heartbreak compared to the tragedy King had suffered? "I've been working them too hard. We'll just quit this afternoon and go to the park like you—"

"Ellie, tell *Mitch* you love him."

"*Mitch?* But I don't love—"

"I may be handicapped, Ellie, but I'm not stupid. You've been listening to this tape all week. I know what love looks like, and Mitch loves you as much as you love him.''

Ellie stood up. Moved away from King. ''Mitch doesn't love me.''

''Ellie, I set a bad example for him. He just doesn't know what to do with love. You're going to have to show him.''

She turned to him in disbelief. ''Show him? In case you haven't noticed, the man isn't here anymore.''

King just smiled. ''He'll be back.''

I don't think so.

Ellie leaned down to kiss him on the cheek. ''Thank you for sharing. You're a dear, wonderful man, and I *do* love *you*. Now I'm going to follow your advice and take my kids to the park while *you* listen to the tape.''

Spotting a paper flower on the floor, she swept it up and laid it on the bed where Mitch had slept while he'd been here. A useless gesture, she warned herself. She shouldn't hold out hope that Mitch might still come back.

But she knew her heart wasn't listening.

Chapter Eleven

"Last day of school, boys. Have fun. Come straight home." *So you can help me get King to the doctor,* Ellie added silently as she waved her sons off to the bus stop. She wasn't about to remind them of King's appointment and risk stirring memories of Mitch. She didn't want to spoil their last day of school.

Tugging down her oversize Because I'm The Mom T-shirt, she dashed back up the stairs and hurried to the kitchen. Getting the boys smoothly off to school had been an amazing feat this morning. They hadn't argued once, and they'd each brought her a paper flower before they'd left.

She gazed down at the new blossoms in the basket on the counter. Her wonderful sons. Sometimes they managed to act truly angelic. But the flowers stirred painful memories, too—of that first morning her boys had encountered Mitch. They'd been so wary and defensive. So had she. With good reason.

From the counter, she collected the cereal bowls and

stacked them into the dishwasher. The dishwasher that worked—thanks to Mitch.

Darn.

Where was that list? She tore the top sheet from the yellow pad on the counter and read it with resolve.

Boys to school—take flowers for teachers
Open store—give Robin instructions
Seri to day care
Register for dental hygiene classes—junior college
King to doctor— 3:30
Not think about Mitch....

Marking through "Boys to school," she reminded herself to forget about Mitch, then carried the list to the Mermaid Room where she and Seri had settled in again.

Farther down the hall she heard Harriet in the dormitory talking King through his morning physical therapy. Thank goodness Harriet would be here this afternoon to help with the trip to the doctor.

Ellie moved toward the closet, then did a double take. Well, look at that. Seri must have caught the same strange illness her brothers suffered this morning. The bed was already made!

It was nice that her children were behaving so angelically, but something about it bothered her. Her mother sensors still registered Vigilance.

She smoothed a hand across the rumpled bedspread, then frowned. Pulling the spread back, she discovered a scattering of flowers! Seri had left a half-dozen paper flowers in the middle of the bed.

The same bed where Ellie had discovered Mitch that first night.

Darn!

Scooping up the flowers, she deposited them in the pile where Seri's raggedy stuffed animals slept, then straightened the spread and turned to the closet.

The space looked gapingly vacant. So many of her clothes were in the laundry or needed some kind of repair. Hurrying back to the kitchen, she pulled out the mending basket, then dropped to her knees. What was a *flower* doing in her mending basket?

With shaking fingers, she picked it up, but what she saw was Mitch—teasing her about her thimble, holding her hands. Kissing her.

Overwhelmed, she sank back on her calves. What had Tinker Bell said to Peter Pan when he didn't understand that she loved him? Something like *You silly goose?* Ellie ought to sew *that* and hang it in every room, because it described her perfectly. She never should have given that flower to Mitch. Now every flower reminded her of him.

Fixing the blossom to the handle of the basket, she found the tunic she wanted and set to stitching the hem. With a vengeance, she bit the thread in two and shoved the basket back into place, then pushed up to go dress. A man's voice jolted her to a stop.

The voice sounded like Mitch.

Suddenly she felt as if she were running through water. Part of her wanted to sprint through the flat, and part of her didn't want to see him at all. She didn't think she could handle another goodbye.

But her feet carried her forward, and the voice grew clearer until she couldn't deny it was his. Struggling to breathe calmly, she stopped outside the door to King's old bedroom, but she couldn't bring herself to look in.

"So Lucy Maloney took her new lawn mower and cut wonderful pictures all through people's lawns. And that's why they call it Lucy Maloney's Magic Mowing Machine." Click.

Click?

Ellie stuck her head around the door frame.

The room was empty except for Seri. She sat in the middle of King's bed in her mermaid nightshirt leaning against her big pink rabbit. Holding a tape recorder.

Ellie's heart plummeted. Mitch wasn't here, after all. It was only a recording. Like mother, like daughter.

"I didn't know Mitch taped a story for you, sweetheart."

Seri started, then hugged the rabbit closer and peeked up at Ellie sideways. "He made it up for me. It's better than a fairy tale," she added defensively.

"I'm sure it is. Maybe sometime you'll let me listen."

Seri bounced up straighter. "Want to listen now?"

Guilt poked Ellie in the chest. "Can't now, sweetheart."

Seri slumped back against the pillows and buried her face in the rabbit.

"But I promise I'll listen tonight. Right now I want you to get dressed. We have to leave as soon as I come back up from the store."

"Umm-mmm." The rabbit's ears flopped unenthusiastically as Seri shook her head.

Ellie pulled herself out of the room, fighting the urge to snuggle in beside her daughter and listen to Mitch's persuasive voice weave a story of his own making. But neither of them needed more reminders. She didn't need more stories.

Back in the Mermaid Room, she changed into the mended aqua tunic and slid into a pair of black leggings. A fast comb through her hair, a swipe of lip gloss and she made her way down the back stairs.

The store seemed cool and silent. She turned on the lights, opened the cash register and straightened merchandise on her way to the front door. Unlocking it, she retraced her steps to open the storage room. She must remember to remind Robin about families wanting to rent instruments for the summer. She flipped on the light and stepped inside. And caught her breath.

Her hand flew to her throat. The music stand Mitch had used for the KirkKnoll concert stood in the middle of the room. Poised on its ledge sat a light blue, tissue-paper flower.

Ellie slowed to impatient, mincing steps while she waited for the automatic exit door of the pharmacy to lumber open. If her kids were trying to send her a message, they sure had managed to get her attention.

Flowers. Flowers *everywhere*. Her kids had decided to haunt her with them—it was the only explanation she could think of. Her children were refusing to let her forget Mitch. They were telling her what she'd told them at least a bazillion times: actions speak louder than flowers.

But that was silly. Her kids didn't even know she'd given Mitch a flower. She was just overreacting, finding hidden meanings where there were none. Because of the realization that had haunted her all week—if she really loved Mitch, she should do something.

Maybe she should. Maybe she should take a chance, tell him her feelings, follow King's advice. Show Mitch what to do about love. But how could she, when he wasn't even here? When she didn't know if King was right. So many things Mitch had done while he'd been here had been acts of love. But he'd never told her he loved her.

Zigzagging through the half-open door, Ellie hurried to the car. She tossed the package on the opposite seat and quickly reviewed her list, marking through "Seri to day care," "Register for dental hygiene classes," and the hastily scrawled request King had made as she'd been going out the door—"pick up RX at pharmacy."

She'd probably never be able to check off *"Not think about Mitch,"* but she'd better hurry if she was going to check off "King to doctor—3:30." The pharmacy stop had her running late.

The engine started with a roar, and she pulled the rental car onto KirkKnoll Road. At the light, she turned onto a side street. Halfway down the block, she caught sight of a scattering of litter along the roadside. Very white litter. Her foot jerked from the accelerator.

Not more flowers! Anxiously she slowed. No, just paper. She breathed a sigh of relief, caught herself half grinning even as she shook her head in disapproval. Apparently kids hadn't changed. They still confettied the world with old school papers in celebration of the summer to come.

Her boys were probably already home from school. She'd better hurry to corral them before they took off to play.

Around another corner, onto the familiar tree-lined street, here less littered with paper, but... Some of that paper looked an awful lot like... She braked the car, leaned out the window, squinted...

A *flower*. That was *definitely* a pink tissue flower. And *there*, another. This one pale green. And ahead, there were *more*. Tissue flowers, their *love* flowers, scattered all along the sidewalk.

Ellie's foot hit the accelerator. She'd known her sons weren't angels. She could forgive them a few jubilantly tossed school papers. But not this. Not the flowers they'd taken to give their teachers. This time they'd gone too far.

She followed the growing trail up the street, trying to curb her distress. Why would they do such a thing? This looked like open rebellion. How was she going to deal with them?

Parking opposite the store, she crossed to the sidewalk following the flowers that lay, almost like a path, all the way to the flat's front door.

Like a path...? Ellie stopped. Like in a story? She looked up at the windows above the store. The curtains were drawn. Something very strange was going on. Something very strange *indeed!*

She stepped into the entryway, half expecting to find more flowers, and finding them...everywhere! Flowers on the floor, flowers on the stair railings, flowers stuck to the walls—and lying on every stair, all the way to the top.

Then she was on the steps, bounding upward as fast as she could go, with no idea what to expect except that something very strange was happening, something unexplained and a little frightening...and surely magical.

At the landing, she stopped, unable to move except to breathe in the incredible fragrance and shake her head in wonder. The whole room blossomed with flowers, *real* flowers—bouquets of daisies and daffodils and tulips, vases of red roses and pink roses and peach. Flowers, flowers, flowers everywhere; the flat was awash in their perfumes.

She'd just arrived in heaven. It had to be heaven, because here were her very own laughing angels, Gabe and Michael and Rafe, and Seri, too, grabbing her by the hands, tugging her into the room, chanting "We love you, we love you,'' accompanied by the barking of a silly little dog with a ring of daisies around her neck. And off to the side, King in his wheelchair with Harriet beside him, chanting, too. Making Ellie laugh and cry all at the same time.

And then... There was Mitch.

He stood in the doorway to the kitchen, his arms laden with white roses, his mouth tugged into that almost-smile, his eyes... Omigod, those sapphire eyes. So apprehensive. So scared! He took her breath away.

"Ellie—" He faltered.

As if in a dream, she watched Rafe—her quiet, meek little Rafe—grab Mitch's arm and tug him into the room. "Go on, tell her. Aren't you going to tell her?"

"Rafe, where are your—?"

"It's okay, Ellie." Mitch's ruddy tan deepened. "He just wants me to tell you what I already told them. The whole time I was gone, I couldn't get this bunch of hooligans out of my mind. I...missed you. I wanted you with me."

His words came hard, but his gaze never left hers. She could see these were things he had to say, no matter how difficult. She rested her palms on Seri's shoulders to calm her excitement. To keep her own hands from trembling.

"While I was here, you kept reminding me of the good times we had when *I* was a kid. As a family. But after my mother died, I couldn't let go of that kid's anger.

"Then Seri ran away, and you showed me...how to forgive."

He stepped into the room. Put one hand on his father's shoulder. Ellie saw the look that passed between them.

No longer tense and angry, but hopeful. Tinged with love. Willing to try. Her heart filled with joy.

"You showed me something else, Ellie." From among the roses, he held up a tissue flower, like the one she'd given him. "You showed me you were willing to risk loving *again*."

Seri couldn't wait any longer. She grabbed Ellie's hand and tugged her forward. "Come on, Mommy, kiss him. He loves us. He wants to marry us."

"Marry? Us?" Ellie stalled in her tracks. Mitch looked a little panicked, but that didn't stop his smile from curling into a grin.

"Hey, Princess, that was supposed to be my line." He moved nearer, still cradling the roses. Still looking half ready to bolt and run.

It came to her then that if she took a few steps, the top of her head would just brush his chin—at least a second or two before she reached up for his kiss. Holding her ground was the hardest thing she'd ever done.

"The thing is, Ellie, I can buy into Winterhaven with Jack and make a pretty good living. And the house I was renovating would make a great home. For a family, I mean. There's a college not too far away, too—with a dental program. But...well, maybe you've come to your senses. Maybe you don't want to take another chance."

For just a second, she hesitated. Did she? Could she promise her heart to a man who had kept his own locked away so long? Was *he* ready to risk caring about someone again?

"Look, Ellie, I know Colorado sounds like just another gig. How about if I move back to KirkKnoll? Get a job here. Be home every night. Marry me, Ellie. Your kids have already said *they* will."

"Yes, yes, yes!" Seri, Michael and Rafe danced

around her in a circle. But Gabe stood silently to one side.

Ellie felt torn in two. Mitch hadn't told her he loved her. And her son—she thought he'd accepted Mitch, but now...

"Wait." Ellie put her hands on her children again, this time to give her strength. "What do *you* say, Gabe?"

Gabe drew himself up, folded his arms across his chest, tucked in his chin. "I say...no."

No? Was he testing *her* faithfulness as a parent? Asking her to choose?

"Honey, can you tell me why?"

"Yeah." His defiant gaze slid to Mitch. "We want to live in Colorado. We want to help Mitch fix up his house. We want to ride the school bus in the mountains and learn how to ski."

"So you're saying, *if we went to Colorado* you wouldn't mind if I...if we married him?"

Gabe's defiance faded. He searched Mitch's face, looking almost as worried as Mitch. "I guess...if he *really* loves us, we could live here, too."

Ellie's throat tightened. Tears blossomed in her eyes. That was pretty much the way she felt.

In two long strides, Mitch closed the distance between them. He hugged the bouquet of white roses—there must have been three dozen or more—looking remarkably relieved. "These are for you, Ellie. I haven't had any practice...and the flowers say it a lot better. But I love you, Ellie."

She wanted to kiss him, she wanted to climb into his arms and never come out. But darn him, the man still clutched an armload of thorny white roses! King was right—she'd have to show him about love.

Reaching up, she lifted one white rose from the fragrant mass, then laid the rest on the sofa. She slid the rose through the buttonhole of his shirt. Like a boutonniere for a wedding.

"I love you, Mitch. And I think I just got the go-ahead for a wedding!"

Gabe snorted. "This is gonna get mushy, isn't it?"

Mitch grinned down at Ellie. "Yeah, real mushy."

At last. He folded her in his arms, and she barely heard her thundering crew charge out of the room, hardly registered Harriet's and King's happy laughter as they followed. She gave herself wholly to the kisses she'd resisted and dreamed of and longed for. To Mitch's gentleness, his strength, his hunger. To her Prince Charming.

"We're marrying The Prince, we're marrying The Prince," Seri sang somewhere nearby. "Hey, King, I think this is a happy ending."

Ellie smiled up at Mitch.

"I think it's a happy beginning, too."

Epilogue

"Is everyone finally settled?" Mitch asked, pulling Ellie through the oak-framed doorway of their newly renovated master bedroom and into his arms.

She raised on tiptoes for his kiss. One progressed to two, then three. Pretty soon she lost count. At last she came up for air. It was sweet with the fragrance of the flowers on the dresser.

"Mmm, I think so."

"Think so what?" Mitch murmured, nuzzling the sensitive place at the base of her neck, tugging her toward the king-size bed that dominated the far wall.

"I think everyone's settled." She savored the tingles trailing across her shoulders. "Your dad made it all the way to the guest room with Harriet's help and that walking stick you gave him. Bet he marries Harriet before the year is—"

Mitch's mouth settled over hers and the rest of the thought flew away. Lost in Mitch's arms, she floated across the floor toward the bed, surrendering to his caresses, to the kisses he nibbled down her throat toward the opening of her filmy robe.

A loud thump stopped them both. "Mmm, you tuck in the kids?" she mumbled, seeking his mouth again.

"And the dog. All tucked and properly threatened." He kissed her soundly. "No disturbances on wedding night or no skiing lessons come first snow."

Ellie almost giggled. "This is the strangest wedding night I've ever heard of. More like a family reunion."

Mitch leaned down and scooped her into his arms. "If all we do is talk about it, the sun will come up and Jack and your father will be knocking at the door wanting to talk about Winterhaven's finances. I could hardly get either of them to say good-night!"

This time Ellie did giggle. "And Josey and my mother will be ready to go wildflower hunting with books and grandkids in tow. Mom's so happy she finally got to plan a wedding."

"Ah, but I have plans, too." He waggled his eyebrows, then set Ellie down on the bed and began untying her sash. "I have something for you that I think will make you feel *ve-ry* good."

Ellie reached up to blow in his ear. "I have something for you, too," she whispered. She slid the robe from her shoulders, then tried to pull him down beside her.

"Ah, ah, ah. Not so fast." He held out his hand. In it lay a box. "I told you I had something for you." He grinned wickedly.

"I had something else in mind."

"So do I, so hurry and open it!"

Quickly she untied the gold ribbon and lifted the lid. "Oh, Mitch!"

Inside lay a pair of gold earrings, tiny gold flowers,

just like her paper flowers, only magically, wondrously smaller. A diamond winked from the center of each.

"They're beautiful!"

"They're 'I love you' flowers, Ellie. I'll love you forever."

Just before Ellie reached to kiss him, she saw moonlight flash from the diamonds. Or was it the light of Tinker Bell's glow? Because Mitch had shown her she still believed, after all. Fairy tales really could come true.

* * * * *

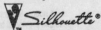

If you enjoyed what you just read,
then we've got an offer you can't resist!

Take 2 bestselling
love stories FREE!
Plus get a FREE surprise gift!

Clip this page and mail it to Silhouette Reader Service™

IN U.S.A.
3010 Walden Ave.
P.O. Box 1867
Buffalo, N.Y. 14240-1867

IN CANADA
P.O. Box 609
Fort Erie, Ontario
L2A 5X3

YES! Please send me 2 free Silhouette Romance® novels and my free
surprise gift. Then send me 6 brand-new novels every month, which I will
receive months before they're available in stores. In the U.S.A., bill me at the
bargain price of $2.90 plus 25¢ delivery per book and applicable sales tax, if
any*. In Canada, bill me at the bargain price of $3.25 plus 25¢ delivery per book
and applicable taxes**. That's the complete price and a savings of over 10% off
the cover prices—what a great deal! I understand that accepting the 2 free
books and gift places me under no obligation ever to buy any books. I can
always return a shipment and cancel at any time. Even if I never buy another
book from Silhouette, the 2 free books and gift are mine to keep forever. So why
not take us up on our invitation. You'll be glad you did!

215 SEN CNE7
315 SEN CNE9

Name	(PLEASE PRINT)	
Address	Apt.#	
City	State/Prov.	Zip/Postal Code

* Terms and prices subject to change without notice. Sales tax applicable in N.Y.
** Canadian residents will be charged applicable provincial taxes and GST.
  All orders subject to approval. Offer limited to one per household.
  ® are registered trademarks of Harlequin Enterprises Limited.

SROM99   ©1998 Harlequin Enterprises Limited

Coming in May 1999

BABY *Fever*

by
New York Times Bestselling Author

KASEY MICHAELS

When three sisters hear their biological
clocks ticking, they know it's
time for action.

But who will they get to father their babies?

Find out how the road to motherhood
leads to love in this brand-new collection.

Available at your favorite retail outlet.

Coming in June 1999 from
Silhouette Books...

Those matchmaking folks at Gulliver's Travels are at
it again—and look who they're working their magic
on this time, in

HOLIDAY Honeymoons

Two Tickets to Paradise

For the first time anywhere, enjoy these two new
complete stories in one sizzling volume!

HIS FIRST FATHER'S DAY   Merline Lovelace
A little girl's search for her father leads her to
Tony Peretti's front door...and leads *Tony* into the
arms of his long-lost love—the child's mother!

MARRIED ON THE FOURTH   Carole Buck
Can summer love turn into the real thing? When
it comes to Maddy Malone and Evan Blake's
Independence Day romance, the answer is a
definite "yes!"

Don't miss this brand-new release—
HOLIDAY HONEYMOONS: Two Tickets to Paradise—
coming June 1999, only from Silhouette Books.

Available at your favorite retail outlet.

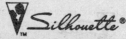

COMING NEXT MONTH

#1372 I MARRIED THE BOSS!—Laura Anthony
Loving the Boss

Sophia Shepherd wanted to marry the ideal man, and her new boss, Rex Michael Barrington III, was as dreamy as they came! But when an overheard conversation had him testing her feelings, Sophia had to prove she wanted more than just a dream....

#1373 HIS TEN-YEAR-OLD SECRET—Donna Clayton
Fabulous Fathers

Ten years of longing were over. Tess Galloway had returned to claim the child she'd thought lost to her forever. But Dylan Minster, her daughter's father and the only man she'd ever loved, would not let Tess have her way without a fight, and without her heart!

#1374 THE RANCHER AND THE HEIRESS—Susan Meier
Texas Family Ties

City girl Alexis MacFarland wasn't thrilled about spending a year on a ranch—even if it meant she'd inherit half of it! But one look at ranch owner Caleb Wright proved it wouldn't be *that* bad, *if* she could convince him she'd be his cowgirl for good.

#1375 THE MARRIAGE STAMPEDE—Julianna Morris
Wranglers & Lace

Wrangler Merrie Foster and stockbroker Logan Kincaid were *nothing* alike. She wanted kids and country life, and he wanted wealth and the city. But when they ended up in a mock engagement, would the sparks between them overcome their differences?

#1376 A BRIDE IN WAITING—Sally Carleen
On the Way to a Wedding

Stand in for a missing bride? Sara Martin didn't mind, especially as a favor for Dr. Lucas Daniels. But when her life became filled with wedding plans and stolen kisses, Sara knew she wanted to change from stand-in bride to wife forever!

#1377 HUSBAND FOUND—Martha Shields
Family Matters

Single mother Emma Lockwood needed a job...and R. D. Johnson was offering one. Trouble was, Rafe was Emma's long-lost husband—and he didn't recognize her! Could she help him recover his memory—and the love they once shared?